KILLER FAKE

Deets realized they were both suspicious, and Mitt's hand was creeping toward his sidearm. Time to show his hole card, Deets decided.

"Well, Mitt," he remarked casually, "you picked a lonely grave."

It took less than two seconds to shuck out his Colt and spray Mitt's blood and brains all over the rocks behind him. The body flopped forward, toes scratching the dirt a few times. Deets swung the still-smoking muzzle toward Louise. She had frozen in place, still lifting the coffeepot off the flames. She was too shocked to scream, staring at her husband's body in horrified disbelief.

"Set that pot down, beauty," he told her in a voice that brooked no defiance. "Then shuck out of them clothes. You're about to meet Skye Fargo in the flesh."

THE

TRAILSMAN

#361

UTAH DEADLY DOUBLE

by

Jon Sharpe

A SIGNET BOOK

SIGNET
Published by New American Library, a division of
Penguin Group (USA) Inc., 375 Hudson Street,
New York, New York 10014, USA
Penguin Group (Canada), 90 Eglinton Avenue East, Suite 700, Toronto,
Ontario M4P 2Y3, Canada (a division of Pearson Penguin Canada Inc.)
Penguin Books Ltd., 80 Strand, London WC2R 0RL, England
Penguin Ireland, 25 St. Stephen's Green, Dublin 2,
Ireland (a division of Penguin Books Ltd.)
Penguin Group (Australia), 250 Camberwell Road, Camberwell, Victoria 3124,
Australia (a division of Pearson Australia Group Pty. Ltd.)
Penguin Books India Pvt. Ltd., 11 Community Centre, Panchsheel Park,
New Delhi - 110 017, India
Penguin Group (NZ), 67 Apollo Drive, Rosedale, North Shore 0632,
New Zealand (a division of Pearson New Zealand Ltd.)
Penguin Books (South Africa) (Pty.) Ltd., 24 Sturdee Avenue,
Rosebank, Johannesburg 2196, South Africa

Penguin Books Ltd., Registered Offices:
80 Strand, London WC2R 0RL, England

First published by Signet, an imprint of New American Library,
a division of Penguin Group (USA) Inc.

First Printing, November 2011
10   9   8   7   6   5   4   3   2   1

The first chapter of this book previously appeared in *Texas Lead Slingers,* the three
hundred sixtieth volume in this series.

Copyright © Penguin Group (USA) Inc., 2011
All rights reserved

 REGISTERED TRADEMARK—MARCA REGISTRADA

Printed in the United States of America

The Trailsman

Beginnings . . . they bend the tree and they mark the man. Skye Fargo was born when he was eighteen. Terror was his midwife, vengeance his first cry. Killing spawned Skye Fargo, ruthless, cold-blooded murder. Out of the acrid smoke of gunpowder still hanging in the air, he rose, cried out a promise never forgotten.

The Trailsman they began to call him all across the West: searcher, scout, hunter, the man who could see where others only looked, his skills for hire but not his soul, the man who lived each day to the fullest, yet trailed each tomorrow. Skye Fargo, the Trailsman, the seeker who could take the wildness of a land and the wanting of a woman and make them his own.

*Utah Territory, 1859—
where a ruthless master of disguise turns Fargo
into the most wanted man in the West.*

1

"Gentlemen," announced the young drummer from Pennsylvania, "there seems to be something a mite queer about this game."

An ominous silence followed his remark. The other four poker players, including Skye Fargo, swiveled their heads to stare at him.

"No offense intended," the salesman hastened to add.

"Well, plenty taken, you mouthy jackanapes," growled Billy Williams, who was assisting Fargo on a scouting mission for the much-ballyhooed Pony Express, due to be launched next year. He scowled darkly and scraped his chair back to clear his gun hand.

"H'ar now!" cautioned Red Robinson from behind the crude plank bar. The burly, redheaded Irishman owned the only saloon—actually just a primitive grog shop—permitted at Fort Bridger by the Mormon Council in Salt Lake City. "Stay your hand, Old Billy. This ain't Laredo. These soldiers in the Mormon Battalion are no boys to mess with. The last gentile who cracked a cap in this puke-hole spent three months in the stockade."

"Come down off your hind legs, Old Billy," Fargo threw in, strong white teeth flashing through his neatly cropped beard as he grinned. "Mr. Brubaker here didn't accuse any of us. He simply pointed out there's something a mite queer about the game."

"That's what the lawyers call tantamount to an accusation," chimed in Lemuel Atkins, a Mormon doctor at Fort Bridger who often violated the social order to indulge his love of pasteboard thrills with gentiles, the Mormon word for anyone outside their religion.

"Tanny mount, my hinder," the hotheaded Billy fumed. "Let's kill the young pup with a knife, then, and go snooks on his money. He's called all of us cheaters, ain't he?"

"Not quite," said the fifth player at the table, Sy Munro, an outfitter for pilgrims passing through Fort Bridger on their way to the Sierra goldfields and coast settlements. He wore new range clothes and a clean neckerchief. "I'd say he just implied it."

"Imply a cat's tail!" protested Old Billy. "You heard the doc—it was tanny mount! The snivelin' little scrote called every last one of us cheaters."

"If he did," put in Fargo calmly, shifting a skinny Mexican cigar to the other side of his mouth, "he spoke straight-arrow. Matter of fact, he's the only one at the table who *ain't* cheating. It's him ought to shoot us."

Every jaw at the table dropped, including Lonny Brubaker's.

"Fargo," warned Old Billy, "you *had* teeth when you got here."

Fargo ignored his blustering partner, looking at the dumbfounded drummer. "Mr. Brubaker, have you ever heard of the cheater's table?"

"The . . . no, sir."

"It's a custom that started on the Mississippi riverboats. When trade is slow for the professional gamblers, they get up a game among themselves to hone their cheating skills."

"You mean I just happened along when one of those games was going on here?"

"We're not professionals," Fargo conceded, "but we figured to have a little fun. Old Billy has been crimping cards, Sy smudging them with his cigar, and Doc Atkins has been dealing from every place *except* the top of the deck."

"How 'bout you?"

Fargo grinned. "Every time the doc blew cigar smoke in your face, you turned in my direction and showed me your cards—which ain't cheating, by the way. Learn to cover your cards, son."

Brubaker's smooth-shaven face looked astounded. "Well, I'm clemmed!"

"How much did you drop tonight?" Fargo added.

"Well, twelve dollars."

Fargo counted out three silver dollars from his pile and slid them to Brubaker. "C'mon, boys," he called to the others. "Time to post the pony."

Old Billy loosed a string of epithets worthy of a stable sergeant. Fargo's partner on this Pony Express assignment was a homely cuss with a twice-broken nose and a large birthmark coloring the left side of his face reddish purple. He was still in his thirties but had earned the moniker Old Billy because of his full mane of white-streaked hair—a legacy of nearly twenty years spent fighting some of the most bellicose tribes of the Southwest and Far West. His widespread reputation as an Indian fighter convinced Fargo to get him on the payroll.

"Fargo," he said in a tone heavy with disgust, "the hell's got into you—religion?"

"No, Fargo's right," Doc Atkins said as he counted out three dollars. "I never intended to keep the lad's money. Besides, though it's my own people, Red is correct—scratch a Mormon and you'll find a jailer. Best to take the peace road."

"I don't give a damn what you weak sisters do," Old Billy said stubbornly. "A man shouldn't step in something he can't wipe off, and that's what this clabber-lipped greenhorn done. What's next? We powder his butt and tuck him in? I ain't paying back one red cent."

Fargo watched Old Billy with speculative eyes. "Yeah, I've noticed something peculiar about you. You won't spend money except to gamble and make more. Won't even pony up a dime for a beer. I've never seen a bachelor behave like that."

Old Billy averted his eyes. "So I'm a damn miser. No law agin it."

Fargo shook his head and counted another three dollars out of his own money. "Satan won't allow you into hell, Old Billy—afraid you'll take over."

During this exchange no one had noticed when the cowhide flap that served as a door was suddenly thrust aside. The woman who stepped inside the smoky, dimly lit hovel had a pretty face that was creased from worry and suffering—a familiar sight on the frontier. No one noticed her in the murky shadows until the loud click of a mule-ear hammer being thumbed back seized their attention.

Suddenly all eyes were riveted on the steel-eyed woman with a German fowling piece in her hands. No great threat at a distance, up close like this it could shred a man's face—or his sex gear, Fargo thought, noticing she was aiming it right at him and below the belt. Sweat trickled out of his hairline.

"Why, Dot," Lemuel Atkins said, "what in the—?"

"Put a stopper on your gob, Doc," she snapped, never taking her fiery eyes off Fargo. "You with the buckskins and beard—is that your black-and-white pinto tethered outside?"

"It is, ma'am."

"And be your name Fargo?"

The Trailsman nodded, not liking the determined set of her face nor the dangerous turn this trail was taking.

"Then I'm here to kill you, mister."

Old Billy snickered. "See? Like I warned you, Fargo, never tell 'em you'll be right back. Some believe you."

The woman swung the muzzle toward Old Billy. "Shut your filthy sewer, you prairie rat. This is an over-and-under gun, and both barrels shoot. All of you keep that in mind before you play the hero."

"Hero?" Old Billy repeated. "Lady, it's none of my mix. Fargo stepped into this and he can wipe it off."

"Ma'am, I don't even know you," Fargo said, his voice calmer than he felt.

Lemuel spoke up quickly. "Skye Fargo, this is Dorothy Kreeger. Her husband died of snakebite a hundred miles west of South Pass on their way to settle in San Francisco. She has a seventeen-year-old daughter, Ginny, and—"

"Oh, this randy stallion knows Ginny, all right," Dot cut in. "In fact, he raped her not two hours ago in the hayfields just south of here. And then he beat her bloody and sliced up her limbs with that vicious knife in his boot."

Dead silence followed her remark. All eyes turned to Fargo. On the frontier a woman's accusation carried more force than a man's.

"Ma'am," Fargo said, "I don't call women liars, but I do call them mistaken. I'm sorry about your daughter, but I didn't have thing one to do with it. I've not met the lady."

"I'd hardly expect you to sign a confession. That's why I'm going to shoot you. You men sitting close to Fargo—spread out. I've no call to shoot anyone but him."

Red Robinson spoke up. "Dot, you're mighty mistaken. Two hours ago, you say? Couldn't a been Fargo—he's been right here playing poker for the past four hours."

"That's right," Doc Atkins chipped in. "Besides, I've known Fargo for years. He's the last man to commit a crime like that."

"Oh, I'd expect all of you to take his part. He's the famous Trailsman and all men look up to him. You men are pack animals—what's my girl compared to the high-and-mighty Trailsman?"

"Dot, you got that bass ackwards," Sy cut in. "This is the West. Why, President Buchanan himself would be drag-hanged for treating a female that way."

"Lady," spoke up Billy, barely suppressing a smirk, "Skye Fargo is a skunk-bit coyote, all right. Rotten as they come. I'd shoot the son of a buck."

"Heathens and Mormons," she said with bitter contempt. "Thinking this is all a big joke for your pleasure. My girl described her attacker, and this tall galoot fits the description right down to the ground. You—the young fellow closest to Fargo—get clear, I said, or you'll get the balance of these pellets."

Fargo could see that Lonny Brubaker was so scared he'd turned fish-belly white. But he stubbornly shook his head.

"No, ma'am. Mr. Fargo is innocent. He was right here when you say your daughter was accosted."

"Scootch over, Lonny," Fargo said in a take-charge voice. "If Mrs. Kreeger is bound and determined to cut me down in cold blood, no use you getting plugged, too."

"Hold off, Dot," Doc Atkins implored. "Take a good long look at Fargo. Does he really look like the kind of man who'd need to . . . ravish a woman?"

Dorothy did look at Fargo, long and hard. For the first time, a look of uncertainty crossed her features. "He's mighty rugged and handsome," she admitted. "Well-knit, too. I 'spect women flock to him like flies to sugar."

Old Billy didn't like the turn this trail was taking. "Sure, lady, but you know, some men prefer to make it rough with a woman—gets 'em more het up. I'd shoot him."

"I 'spect a man as ugly as you *has* to be rough," she replied. "Only way you can get it."

She looked speculatively at Fargo. "It's no secret that my Ginny likes men. I've heard all the jokes about how she's 'secondhand' and her sheets are always wrinkled. And the Lord knows there's precious few males at Fort Bridger to catch a young girl's eye. A man like you wouldn't have to attack her—unless he was sick in the brain."

"I don't dally with girls," Fargo told her. "Only women. Mrs. Kreeger, I don't doubt Ginny's word. But I'm not the only man on the frontier who wears buckskins. And the black-and-white pinto is no rare horse."

"No, but it is rare to see a white man riding a stallion. Mostly it's only Indians who don't cut their horses."

Fargo nodded. "I can't gainsay that."

"Can you gainsay that Arkansas toothpick in your boot or that brass-frame rifle in your saddle scabbard? What about the close-cropped beard and your black plainsman's hat? Ginny described all of it."

Fargo shrugged helplessly. "All I can tell you, ma'am, is that I'm innocent. Shouldn't we at least go talk to your daughter before you shoot me?"

She considered this for a few moments, and Fargo thought she was wavering. Then her face set itself hard and she shook her head no.

Her finger slipped inside the trigger guard and curled around the trigger. "No," she said, her voice implacable. "I'm going to kill you now before I go weak-kneed."

2

Fargo had not been fooled by Old Billy's remarks egging Dorothy on to kill the Trailsman. He had sided the veteran Indian fighter long enough to know how his mind worked. Those remarks were intended to make her think Old Billy would be the last man to try saving Fargo. In fact, he was the first.

Even as the distraught woman weighed the decision to pull the trigger, Old Billy slid the bolos from his sash unseen. Made of two small lead balls with a short stretch of rope melted into the lead to connect them, bolos were excellent for silently dropping men or animals.

Billy's arm shot out swift as a snake's tongue, and the bolos wrapped hard around Dorothy's ankles, upending her like a ninepin. The fowling piece went off straight up in the air, blowing a hole in the thatch roof. Fargo rocketed out of his chair and caught the woman in both arms before she hit the rammed-earth floor.

He kicked the gun away and started to help her to her feet. She surprised him by breaking into hard, wracking sobs, clinging tight to him. Fargo knew she had hit her breaking point. The recent loss of her husband, this vicious attack on her daughter, and now the two of them alone in a hard, unforgiving land—even a strong man could break in this pitiless country of sterile mountains and jagged canyons and endless purple sage, not to mention some of the most warlike Indians in America.

Nonetheless, Fargo still had a man's animal nature, and this woman was still young enough to feel mighty good through her thin calico dress. He realized she was absolutely buck naked under it, her pliant nipples prodding into his chest as she sobbed. His right hand cupped her hip and he felt the deep-sweeping curve. It had been a while for Fargo, and he was forced to discreetly shift his position on the floor to accommodate his arousal.

Finally she pulled away and stared into Fargo's lake blue eyes.

"It wasn't you," she said, sniffing. "It couldn't have been. As impossible as it seems, it wasn't you."

"I'm glad you've come round to the truth," Fargo told her. "But if it wasn't for Old Billy, I'd be deader than a Paiute grave. And you might have killed Lonny Brubaker, too."

"Hell, that's his fault," Old Billy put in. "Damn fool acting like Lancelot."

Fargo helped the still-shaking woman to her feet. She looked at Doc Atkins. "Are you going to turn me over to the Mormon constable?"

"Why bother? You won't find any place in the West that will jug a woman for anything. You just settle your nerves, Dot. You've had a lot heaped on you."

"Hell," said Billy, who had the anti-Mormon complex, "just send her to Old Brigham in Salt Lake City. That randy old goat has filled two houses with his wives. Might as well add one that ain't ugly as a mud fence."

Atkins narrowed his eyes. "That kind of talk on Mormon soil will get you a taste of the cowhide."

He shifted his gaze to Dorothy. "What about Ginny's wounds? Were they treated?"

She swiped at her eyes and nodded. "I took care of them. I was a nurse back in Arkansas."

Sy Munro pushed to his feet. "Dot, I think we need to talk with Ginny, don't you? Fargo didn't commit this outrage, so we need to find out who did."

The woman nodded. "But do all of you need to come? After what she's been through, she doesn't need a passel of men staring at her."

"Makes sense," Sy agreed. "How 'bout just Fargo and Doc Atkins? Fargo should go so she can get a close-up look at him."

"Send Lancelot, too," Old Billy tossed in, inclining his head toward Lonny Brubaker. "Maybe he can heal her with a kiss."

The three of them headed outside into the hot glare of early-afternoon sunshine. Fort Bridger, located in the extreme northeastern corner of the Utah Territory, was an outpost of Salt Lake City, a stage-relay station, and an important rescue station for Mormons and gentiles alike. Despite its pike-log fence and guard towers, it was not a military fort except for a small detachment of soldiers from the battle-tested Mormon Battalion, first formed in 1846 as volunteers for the bloody war with Mexico.

"My tent is over behind the feed stables," Dot told the men. "It ain't much to look at."

Not much around here was, Fargo thought, even as a harsh gust of wind blew in from the surrounding alkali plain and brought stinging sand with it. The Mormon side of the compound looked a bit more settled, with some plank dwellings and livestock. But the area reserved for gentiles looked more transitory: a motley sprawl of tents, clapboard shebangs, and crude lean-tos made from wagon canvas. A group of men were pitching horseshoes, arm-wrestling, placing small bets on footraces—anything to alleviate the boredom of a desolate way station.

Dot watched Fargo take all of it in as they walked, leaning forward against the wind. "It's a mite dreary, ain't it?"

"Matter of perspective, ma'am. I could show you a buffalo camp called Hog's Breath, back in central Kansas, that makes this place look like St. Louis."

"I do admire the mountains," she added. "They rise up forever."

She meant the rugged Wasatch Range that ran north and south of Fort Bridger. Fargo admired them, too, despite their steep, sterile slopes. Their granite spires wore wispy capes of cloud.

Dot stopped in front of a worn tent that had been patched with leather flaps and sinew. "I best go in first," she told the two men. "Ginny's liable to throw a conniption fit if I just barge in there with Mr. Fargo."

She stepped inside and the Doc looked at Fargo. "Hell of a thing, Skye. I'll have to report this, you know. Too many women and girls here."

Fargo nodded. "No way around it."

"But I'd rather not do it while you're still here. A lot of the Mormons don't know you, and you know how it is when a woman's been outraged—even a gentile. Weren't you and Billy planning on riding out toward Echo Springs in the morning?"

Again Fargo nodded.

"Pathfinding for the Pony?" Atkins used the popular name for the highly sensationalized Pony Express, the latest publicity gimmick of the cash-starved freighting empire of Russell, Majors & Waddell.

Fargo heard a young woman's voice rising in protest from within the darkness of the tent.

"Not actual pathfinding," he told Doc Atkins. "The route has already been laid out. Me and Billy are scouting out locations for the line stations they'll need all along the route. They'll soon have to be built and peopled up if this overland-mail route is to kick off next year."

Atkins shook his head. "Five dollars a letter—hell and damnation! Nobody has that kind of money but prospectors. Anyway, any chance you and Billy might dust your hocks out of here before tomorrow?"

"Good chance," Fargo said, seeing which way the wind set. "First I want to talk with this girl. Something ain't quite jake here."

"It's a poser, all right."

"Gentlemen," came Dot's voice, "come on in."

Fargo had to pause just inside the fly of the tent to let his eyes adjust from the harsh glare outside. Dot lighted a coal-oil lantern and hung it from a hook on the center pole. The tent was crowded with bundles and carpetbags and overflowing crates. Fargo's gaze landed on a striking young woman lying on a blanket roll, staring at him fearfully. Her honey blond hair was fanned out around her head on the blankets.

"Hello, Ginny," Doc Atkins said in a kind voice. "How are you feeling?"

She didn't answer, still staring at Fargo.

"Honey, this is Mr. Skye Fargo," her mother said.

"I know who he is," Ginny replied in a sullen voice. "I . . . met him earlier today."

"Ginny," Fargo assured her, "I've never seen you in my life."

"Ain't *you* a bald-faced liar! Look what you done to me."

Fargo did look. Her pretty face was stained by two grape-colored bruises, one eye nearly swollen shut. Dot pulled her skirt up to show neat swathes of bandages on her thighs.

"No need to pull my skirt up for him," the girl spat out. "He's already done that."

"Ginny," Doc Atkins said, "that's impossible. Fargo has been playing cards with me and three other men for the past four hours. Before that, I saw him shoeing his horse."

"Then he's got a twin brother, Doc," Ginny insisted. "One who wears the same buckskins with old blood on the fringes. And the same hat and beard—and wears a walnut-handle gun and carries a big knife in his boot. You ever seen twins like that?"

Fargo took his hat off and flipped it aside, placing his hands on his knees and leaning closer to the girl. She pulled back.

"Ginny," he said, "I know you're upset, and who could blame you? But take a good look at me—for a full minute just study my face."

Clearly she didn't want to, but neither could she tear her eyes from this handsome man with the calm, compelling manner. Silently, seriously, she scrutinized him.

"The hair," he finally said. "Is it exactly like your attacker's?"

She looked uncertain. "Well . . . his *did* seem to have a bit more curl in it. And just maybe it was a little darker."

"The eyes?"

She squinted. "They was blue but . . . more like a slate blue. Yours look the color of lake water."

"The mouth and beard?"

"The beard was just the same, short and brown and real thick. But the mouth . . . it was meaner somehow, I think."

"What about his build, hon?" Dot coaxed.

"Well . . ." She ran her gaze up and down his length. "He was just as tall, I 'spose. But this man's shoulders look a little wider."

"Are you still sure," Doc Atkins said, "that this is the man who attacked you?"

"I . . . when I take a fast look, yes. But when I go part by part, I can't swear to it."

She sent Fargo a tentative smile. "This man is decent. You can see it in him. The other is the lowest trash though he knows how to hide it."

"Did you hear his voice?" Fargo asked.

She nodded. "It was nice, like yours. Until he got mean."

Fargo retrieved his hat and straightened up. "One last favor, Ginny. In a bit I'll be riding out with my partner. We'll need to know exactly where this attack took place. And may we stop back here so you can take a good look at my horse? I want to know how the two size up."

"Yes. You're going after him, aren'tcha, Mr. Fargo?"

Fargo nodded once. "That I am. I've got a job to do, but I've got a hunch his trail will cross mine."

She looked satisfied. "I've read stuff about you. Kill the son of a bitch."

Fargo's lips twitched into a grin. "He made the call, Ginny. Now it's root hog or die."

With a huge yellow sun starting to wester, Fargo and Old Billy tacked their horses for the trail. Fargo cast an uneasy eye at the knot of men starting to gather around the big livery barn.

"Word's got out about Ginny," Fargo muttered as he tossed on saddle and pad. "Doc Atkins must be taking our side or they'd have collared us by now."

"Doc Atkins, my sweet aunt," Old Billy shot back as he fastened his golden Appaloosa's bridle latch. "These clabber-lipped pilgrims know me and you are death to the devil. *Let* the milk-kneed boardwalkers try to arrest me—there'll be new widows and orphans aplenty."

Fargo's strong white teeth flashed through his beard as he cinched the girth. "Billy, you smell like a whorehouse at low tide and there's nothing but rough sides to your tongue. But I'd rather have you siding me than a whole troop of cavalry."

"This from a man who needed to be saved from a woman. Christ, Fargo, do children bully you, too?"

Fargo swung up onto the hurricane deck and wheeled the Ovaro around. Some of the faces were growing uglier as a few drunk gentiles worked them into a white-hot fever.

Fargo jerked the Henry from his saddle boot and jacked a round into the chamber. "If any of you boys are feeling froggy," he invited, "go ahead and jump."

Billy followed suit, pulling out his Greener 12-gauge express gun. "My name is Old Billy Williams," he announced in his rasping voice, "I'm strong as horseradish and I like to kill—goddamn if I don't. I double hog-tie *dare* any of you to make a play. Ain't one of you spineless sons of bitches fit to wipe my ass, and I can send twenty of you across the mountains quick as a hungry man can eat a biscuit."

Fargo knew that wasn't an empty boast. Like most Indian fighters who worked alone, Old Billy was a walking arsenal. Besides the Greener for close-in work, he toted around a seven-shot Spencer carbine. For more personal encounters he wore a fancy repeater made by Brasher of London with ivory grips and a folding knife under the barrel. When it was do or die, he resorted to the double-bladed Cherokee hatchet in his legging sash.

"Williams, the hell you doing takin' the part of a rapist?" demanded a surly, anonymous voice.

"Rape?" Fargo laughed. "There's Mormon soldiers here. You think they'd let me ride out if I raped a woman? Sell your ass, you damn fool."

A few of the men nodded at this logic and drifted off. Fargo and Billy gigged their horses in the direction of the gentile camp.

"Fargo, this hombre that looks like you is trouble," Old Billy opined. "We need to find the bastard and irrigate his guts."

"God's truth, old son. But we also signed a contract with a tight deadline. There's a good piece of country ahead of us yet before we reach Sacramento—the hardest piece, too."

"Uh-huh. You think this Pony Express will ever show color?"

Fargo snorted, making the Ovaro prick up his ears. "It was never meant to. I talked to William Russell and Alexander Majors myself back in St. Louis. They admitted the whole thing will sink in less than a year."

"Christ! Then why take it out of the gate?"

"You know how it is out West. The competition for

freighting contracts is fierce. At one time Russell, Majors, and Waddell had the whole range to themselves. Now Overland, Creighton, and other haulers are cutting off much of the grass. The Pony is creating plenty of hoopla, and they're hoping to be the big men on the totem pole once more."

Billy shook his head in disgust. "It's like wasting water to make it rain. Well, long as we get *our* shiners."

By now they'd trotted their mounts to the front of the Kreeger tent.

"Mrs. Kreeger," Fargo called as he swung down, holding the reins. "Is Ginny up to coming outside?"

"We're on our way, Mr. Fargo."

"That Dot Kreeger is a fine specimen of woman flesh," Billy muttered from the saddle. "You gonna trim her, Fargo?"

"Pleasant as that might be," Fargo replied, "all I want right now is to show this place my dust."

The two women emerged, blinking in the bright sunlight.

"Lord," Old Billy whispered, "yoke the two of 'em and we'll work as a team."

"I have good ears, sir," Dorothy Kreeger said.

"Beg pardon, ma'am," Old Billy said. "I'll launder my talk."

"Better yet," Fargo told him, "don't talk at all, you chucklehead."

He turned to Ginny, who was leaning on her mother. "Is this the same horse you saw earlier? Take your time and look close."

She did, hobbling around the Ovaro for a complete study.

"Well, they sure do look powerful similar," she finally said. "The color is just right, and so is the saddle. The markings . . . you know how it is with a paint. I can't swear those are alike."

"How 'bout size and shape?" Fargo pressed.

Ginny looked some more. "The two seem as tall. But this horse seems to have more muscle in its . . ."

She pointed.

"Haunches?" Fargo supplied.

"Yes. And this one seems deeper in its chest."

Fargo nodded. "Now, where's the exact spot where you were attacked, Ginny?"

She pointed. "I went out the south gate. There's irrigated fields out there for about a mile. The last two are hayfields divided by the only trail. I was at the edge of the left field when he rode up."

"Was he coming from camp or toward it?"

"Toward it."

Fargo thanked both women and forked leather. As the two men headed for the gate, he realized he had jumped over a snake this time: He had a bulletproof alibi in the form of that poker game.

Next time, Fargo realized, he wouldn't likely be so lucky. And "justice," in the lawless Far West, was usually more swift than certain.

3

Fargo and Old Billy rode the narrow lane side by side through the irrigated fields, Mormon field hands watching them from lidded gazes.

"Word got out fast," Billy remarked. "Looks like you're totin' the no-good label, Fargo."

The Trailsman was relaxed in the saddle but vigilant, his sun-slitted gaze missing nothing.

"Looks that way," he agreed cheerfully. "But if I'm the King Rat, what's that make you for siding me?"

"What I've always been. A low-down, whiskey-suckin', mother-lovin' son of the sagebrush."

"You only suck whiskey when somebody else planks their cash. What do you do with your money, save it for your trousseau?"

"Fargo, give over with all these questions about my money. You best put your brain toward this hombre that's raping and cutting women in your name. Word's bound to spread, you know. We could both end up with our tits in the wringer. I want to finish this job—the wages is damn good."

Fargo conceded all this with a grim nod. "Yeah, that's the deal, all right. It's a mite curious, huh?"

Old Billy popped a horehound candy into his mouth. "Curious? Fargo, a two-headed cow is curious. This here is downright baffling."

Fargo nodded again but said nothing. He held the Ovaro to an easy trot in the wagon-rutted lane. Fort Bridger had been built here to take advantage of a natural plateau suited for cropland. But not far beyond the southern edge of the fields, the rugged Utah landscape took over. Hills, some threatening to become small mountains, were interspersed with wind-scrubbed knolls and lofty mesas. Purple sage formed a moving carpet with waves rolling through it when the wind gusted. The hills dotted with bluebonnets and daisies, the green expanses of buffalo grass, were well behind them now.

"This looks like the spot," he said, drawing rein. "See where the hay was beat down? That's where our mystery man raped Ginny."

"She says she was raped," Billy gainsaid, lighting down and tossing his reins forward. "Wouldn't be the first gal that gave some fellow the go sign and then got in over her head."

"Could be," Fargo agreed. "But she sure as hell didn't give him the go sign to slice her up like a Sunday ham. Besides, I ain't worried so much about that. If she's telling the straight about this jasper's appearance and horse, I'm the one's in a world of shit."

"Could be she *ain't* telling the straight," Old Billy suggested as Fargo went down on his haunches to study the edge of the trail. "Hell, you're famous, Fargo, you old pussy hound. And life around this hole is about as exciting as a bucket of sheep dip. Could be that gal flopped in the hay with some trail tramp who cut her up and made tracks out of here. So she turned him into Skye Fargo to get some attention."

Fargo bent his face even closer to a track that caught his eye. "Nah. Look at it with the bark still on it. Trouble follows me, and trouble follows you. This fellow is real enough, all right. But what's his play?"

Fargo reached into one of the prints and pinched the dirt. "A few hours old, is all. He didn't picket or hobble his mount, just left it half in the hay, half on the trail. His horse's rear offside shoe is a mite loose."

Old Billy, better at cutting sign on Indians than whites, looked puzzled. "How the hell you know that?"

"Look at the print close—you can see it's smudged. A loose shoe will do that."

Fargo began sifting carefully through the flattened hay, searching for clues. His patience paid off when his fingers extracted a small piece of foolscap folded once. He opened it up and read the four-word note before handing it to Old Billy.

"Fargo, you jughead, you know I can't read nor cipher. The hell's it say?"

Fargo glanced at it again. " 'Death's second self, Fargo.' "

Old Billy's homely face puckered with confusion. "That's the whole shootin' match?"

Fargo nodded.

"It's too far north for me. The hell's it mean?"

Fargo heaved a weary sigh and glanced all around them. "It means Ginny was likely telling the truth. And you and me got trouble on our tail."

In the western reaches of the Unitah Mountains, two days' ride northeast of Salt Lake City, lay the crude outpost of Echo Canyon. It was a place most pilgrims avoided, if possible. If not, they crossed their fingers, loaded their weapons, and stayed in groups for self-protection.

It was a double handful of tar-papered shacks and boasted neither hotel nor school nor church. However, there were four grog shops always doing a lively trade. In the most nefarious of these establishments, a trio of rough, unusually pale men sat nursing a bottle of wagon-yard whiskey.

"Well, boys," said Butch Landry, wiping his lips on his sleeve and passing the bottle around, "by now Skye Fargo might be cooling his heels in a Mormon calaboose."

Landry was a compact, powerfully built man who could wrestle a seventeen-hand horse to the ground. His eyes were as black and fathomless as obsidian.

"Don't mention no goddamn calaboose," drawled Harlan Perry, a big, raw-boned man who hailed from the hollows of Tennessee. "Ain't no son of a bitch born of woman ever hauling me to prison again."

"Ease off," Landry said. "We got away clean, didn't we? And if Deets earns his pay, Fargo will soon get a taste of what we ate. Remember, boys, under Mormon law no man can be executed without a year or two in prison for 'penance.' Ain't that the shits?"

As he often did, Landry fell silent and stared at his folded hands atop the table. Their leader, the other two had learned long ago, was a brooder with an explosive temper that made him kill without warning. But when he murdered a federal paymaster in west Texas for taking too long to throw a strongbox down, the U.S. Army hired Skye Fargo to track down the gang.

As if plucking the thoughts from Landry's head, the third man at the table, Orrin Trapp, spoke up. "Of all the swinging dicks in the West, it just had to be Fargo they put on our dust."

"Yeah," Landry said, his face twisted and bitter. "But that son of a bitch is bound for hell."

Fargo had dogged the trio into the rugged Big Bend country near the Rio Grande and trapped them in a rock canyon. In the ensuing shootout, Fargo's Henry sent a .54 caliber slug smashing into the head of Butch's kid brother, Ralston, spraying his brains all over Butch and unnerving the rest. Believing they faced a well-armed posse of Texas Rangers, Butch surrendered.

The three survivors spent the next five years at hard labor in a federal prison in Sedalia, Missouri. But with the help of crooked guards they engineered their escape. And now Butch had made turnabout the mission of his life—gunning Fargo down would be too merciful. With the help of Mormon law and James "Deets" Gramlich, Butch meant to put Fargo in prison before he faced the gallows.

Orrin didn't look too convinced. He had a vulpine face with mistrustful eyes constantly darting like minnows. They stayed in motion now, watching the dozen or so patrons in the dingy watering hole.

"I don't trust this son of a bitch Deets," he complained to Landry. "All that high-blown talk of his. He uses them thirty-five-cent words a man's never heard before. I got no use for a man what talks like a book."

"Katy Christ!" Butch swore at his minion. "Orrin, don't you never look a man in the eye when you talk at him? It unstrings my damn nerves."

However, there was no real venom behind his words. Orrin was an expert with a knife, especially the wide-bladed Spanish dag he carried behind his red sash—Butch had watched him slice a man's torso open at twenty paces, a useful skill when guns weren't practical.

"I don't trust Deets either," Butch admitted. "But so long

as we keep supplying him with yeller boys, he'll walk his chalk. Matter of fact, could be he earned his pay already up at Fort Bridger. We'll know soon enough."

"I sorta cotton to Deets," Harlan Perry chimed in. "And I like the plan you cooked up, Butch. Thanks to the newspapers, everybody knows exactly where Fargo is going to be— tracking the route of the Pony Express. We know exactly where he is, but he don't know from beans where we are. Hell, prob'ly don't even know yet that we busted out."

Butch nodded, grinning with self-satisfaction. "Now you're whistling, Harlan. And that ain't the half of it—*we* don't even have to bust a cap at Fargo and neither does Deets. That slick son of a bitch *is* Fargo now. Won't be long, the worm will turn, boys."

Landry grabbed the bottle and took a sweeping-deep slug from it. "Mark my words—Fargo will rot in a Mormon prison and then dance on air. And we get to watch the whole thing like it was a play—a play just for us."

By the time a bloodred sun blazed its last and disappeared below the horizon, Fargo and Old Billy had pitched camp in the lee of a knoll about fifteen miles south of Fort Bridger. Despite the furnace-hot days it was only early spring, and temperatures varied as much as forty degrees from day to night. The men had dug a fire pit and circled it with rocks, building a fire of dead juniper wood.

Both men carried goatskins of water lashed to their mounts, and they watered their horses from their hats, tying on feedbags of crushed barley—graze was sporadic in northeastern Utah and would get even scarcer. Fargo would use his letter of credit from William Russell to buy more grain and other supplies in Salt Lake City.

"That's mighty fancy scribblin'," Old Billy remarked, watching over Fargo's shoulder. "You ain't had no schooling, Fargo. Where'd you learn to make maps?"

Fargo finished making a curving contour line to pinpoint the last line-station location they had selected, some three miles back. He worked on a piece of broken plank spread across his thighs, sturdy topographical paper flattened against it.

"It's no proper map," he admitted. "I've scouted for the Topographical Corps so many times I picked up some tricks."

"Them there wavy lines you're making—how come they alla sudden go flat in the back?"

"That's to indicate a cliff they can use for protection on one side. And this grid line here shows that embankment we looked at—it can be used as one wall for the station and the livery barn. That's two directions they don't have to worry about being attacked from."

Old Billy poured more coffee from the blue enameled pot sitting near the fire. "Fargo, they hired the right man when they signed you on. You been bustin' your hump to find the safest locations for these line stations."

"That's my job." Fargo looked up at Billy in the flickering firelight. "I don't like this, Billy. I don't like it at all."

"Don't like what? The money, the food, or my company?"

"No, you numbskull, *this*. All these damn line stations spread out ten to fifteen miles apart in the middle of Robin Hood's barn."

"Why, what's your dicker in it? You yourself said the best protection these young, scrawny riders will have is their size and their fresh horses. How they gonna have fresh horses without plenty of line stations?"

"It's not the riders," Fargo protested, "who'll have the most to worry about. They'll be galloping the whole time. But the stations have to be manned—cooks, wranglers, likely a station-master. They'll be sitting ducks for warpath Indians and road gangs. Soldiers and law dogs are scarce as hen's teeth out here."

Billy nodded. "I take your point. But it's none of our mix, Fargo. We got our own spectac'lar dangers to lock horns with. You can't mollycoddle the next man out West. It's every man for himself and the devil take the hindmost."

"Most of that bluster is right," Fargo agreed, "except the 'every man for himself' part. I s'pose you were only looking out for yourself when Dot Kreeger got blood in her eyes and damn near aired me out?"

"Why, hell yes. I flipped the bolos around her on account if she done for you, I'd be out of a good job. I can't make maps nor scout like you."

"Yeah, I forgot about that, you heartless bastard." Fargo returned to his location-and-contour map. But four words kept echoing in memory and dancing across his map:

Death's second self, Fargo.

Old Billy must have been thinking the same thing. "Fargo, you think this yahoo what attacked Ginny actually looks like you, or is he got up to look like you?"

"It would pain me, Billy, to think another man shared these good looks."

Old Billy snorted. "A bunch of *females* are good-looking. You are a vain son of a bitch. I've seen that looking-glass in your saddle pocket."

"If I was as ugly as you, I'd avoid mirrors, too."

"I *like* being ugly. It scares Injuns, and I don't have no jealous husbands trying to hind-end me with buckshot just because their woman looks at me. Say . . . speaking of good-looking females, that Dot Kreeger and her girl is both easy to look at. Happens I had my choice, I'd park my boots under the old lady's bed. She's built like a Lancaster wagon."

Fargo had to agree. She was built so fetchingly, in fact, that he was convinced she was wearing a corset. But she had been naked under that dress.

"Let's change the subject," Fargo suggested. "I'm woman-starved lately."

"All right, then. I take it you noticed them featherheads watching us from a distance while we looked over that last line-station location?"

Fargo nodded. "Utes, right?"

"Utes. You can always tell them far off on account they got no topknot and they always stand sideways to whatever they're watching."

Fargo stretched his back. "Couldn't've been a war party or they would have attacked us."

"Nah. The Mormons have pacified them with all sorts of presents and such. Still, they bear watching. There's rene-gade bands around."

"Damn straight," Fargo said. "I tangled with a couple of them in the Salt Desert."

"I've locked horns with more than a couple," Billy said. "I won't rate the Ute warrior as high as an Apache or Comanche, but they are six sorts of trouble. Mayhap we best do turnabout on guard tonight. I'll roust you when the pole star is high."

Billy farted loudly. "Whoa! Did an angel speak? Kiss for ya, Fargo."

Fargo laid his Henry beside his bedroll, unbuckled his gun belt, and crawled into his blanket, laying his head on his saddle. But as he waited for sleep to claim him, he thought back on the trouble so far. He and Billy had barely survived scrapes along the North Platte and Sweetwater Rivers as well as a set-to with Teton Sioux where the Green River and Mormon Trail met.

And the worst was yet to come in the vast Utah Territory's imposing mountains and deserts. Fargo watched the fiery explosion of stars overhead and thought about the fear in Ginny's eyes when he went inside that tent. No two ways about it, he thought—he would soon be trapped between a sawmill and a shootout.

4

On the morning after the incident at Fort Bridger, James "Deets" Gramlich sat his pinto stallion atop a long ridge overlooking the freight road to Salt Lake City. For a half hour he had been monitoring the slow progress of a sturdy four-in-hand prairie schooner headed due west from the direction of South Pass.

He had not seen it during his quick reconnoiter of Fort Bridger on the night before the attack on Ginny Kreeger—meaning they were probably well-stocked and didn't waste time cutting north to the fort. Or so Deets hoped. The less they knew, the better.

He pulled a small telescope from his saddlebag and got a better look at the man and woman on the leather-padded springboard seat. Deets loosed an appreciative whistle as he examined the woman. A crisp linen bonnet could not disguise her healthy mass of red curls nor the wing-shaped eyes and delicately carved cheekbones.

"General Taylor," he announced to his horse, "Skye Fargo got lucky yesterday, but now the good fortune is all mine."

Deets switched his view to the man driving the wagon and decided to play this real careful. The fellow looked strong and well-armed, wearing a brace of pistols—a smart idea out here. What the hell were they doing traveling alone—were they moon crazy? After the failure yesterday at Fort Bridger, Deets considered this turn in the trail a killer's cornucopia.

He took up the reins and wheeled around behind the ridge, deciding it would be best to meet the couple head-on. He spurred the black-and-white stallion to a lope, then to a gallop, not reining down toward the road until a sharp bend would hide him and his dust. He threaded his way through a tumble of boulders and hit the road traveling east.

By the time he had spotted them, they had pulled into a little juniper thicket to cook a meal and water the team. Deets slowed to a trot. Seeing a rider approach, the man stepped out to the road with his right palm resting on the butt of a Remington repeater.

Deets reined in and flashed a smile through his close-cropped beard. "Hallo, stranger. Mighty queer place to be traveling on your own."

"For a fact," the man agreed, eyeing him closely. "The party we were with up and decided, back at South Pass, to join a group on the Oregon Trail. But that would take us way the hell north of the Sierra goldfields. We've got one of Lansford Stratton's maps showing the southern route to the Humboldt River, so we struck out on our own."

Damn fools, Deets gloated. He had sold a few of those worthless maps himself. They showed water holes and good graze west of Salt Lake City that didn't exist—just endless salt desert. These two were marked for carrion anyway—he'd be doing them a favor. But the woman, when he was done with her, would have to live.

"The name's Mitt Tipton," the man volunteered, shading his eyes to see the rider better. "This here is my wife, Louise. We hail from Bucks County, Pennsylvania. I'm a cooper by trade, and when I heard of the need for barrels in the goldfields, I figured I might as well start my own cooperage there."

While he spoke, the man had been studying Deets with an attention the latter was beginning to enjoy. It was one of those your-name's-on-the-tip-of-my-tongue looks. Now Louise Tipton stepped forward, flashing a mouthful of pretty white teeth.

Deets said, "My name—"

"Is Skye Fargo," she finished for him in an excited tone. "Mitt, recall that picture I showed you from *Putnam's Monthly*? This man's the spitting image."

"Why, so he is! The buckskins, the black-and-white stallion, the beard—why, this is an honor, Mr. Fargo! Won't you light down and have some coffee and scrapple with us?"

"It'd be a pleasure," Deets said, swinging down and leading

the pinto into the juniper thicket. "I've been pounding a saddle since sunup and I'm famished."

Louise dished him up a heaping plate of food and poured him a cup of coffee. Deets sat on a small boulder and tied into the piping hot food.

"Say," Mitt remarked, "we read in the last newspaper we saw that you was working for the Pony Express out here."

Deets swallowed and nodded, watching the shapely wife. "That's right. But me and my pard, Old Billy, had a little set-to west of here with road agents. Billy's caught a bullet in his leg and it's too deep for me to dig out. So I'm headed to Fort Bridger. They got a sawbones there."

Mitt looked surprised. "Your partner is wounded? Maybe we shouldn't've delayed you."

Deets waved this off with one hand. "Aw, he's fine. I got the bleeding under control."

Mitt and his wife exchanged an uneasy glance. This cavalier attitude didn't seem consistent with their notion of the Trailsman.

"I bought a nickel novel about you," Mitt admitted sheepishly. "The writer claimed it was all gospel, but of course it was colored up some."

"They all are," Deets said with his mouth full. "Most of these writers never set foot outside the States."

"This one was about you corralling some gang in Arkansas. There was this Choctaw Indian siding you—a comical fellow who collected white man's writing. Said there was medicine in the letters."

"Oh, yeah," Deets said vaguely. "I recall all that."

"The hell was that Indian's name?" Mitt added. "I always forget."

"Oh, that was Swift Canoe."

A cloud passed over Mitt's strong, square face. "No, I recall now—he was called Cranky Man."

Deets didn't look up from his plate. "That was just his book name. It sounds more colorful than Swift Canoe."

Louise studied the new arrival's face. "It's curious. The newspapers and magazines can't mention often enough your 'light blue eyes the color of a mountain lake.' But your eyes are dark blue—almost slate gray."

Deets set his plate down and wiped his mouth on his sleeve. "Ahh, those scribblers are all frustrated novelists. They make it up as they go along. Some even give me a wife and kids."

Deets realized they were both suspicious, and Mitt's hand was creeping toward his sidearm. Time to show his hole card, Deets decided.

"Well, Mitt," he remarked casually, "you picked a lonely grave."

It took less than two seconds to shuck out his Colt and spray Mitt's blood and brains all over the rocks behind him. The body flopped forward, toes scratching the dirt a few times. Deets swung the still-smoking muzzle toward Louise. She had frozen in place, still lifting the coffeepot off the flames. She was too shocked to scream, staring at her husband's body in horrified disbelief.

"Set that pot down, beauty," he told her in a voice that brooked no defiance. "Then shuck out of them clothes. You're about to meet Skye Fargo in the flesh."

By early afternoon the glaring sun beat down ferociously on Fargo and Old Billy. Fargo had already selected locations for two more line stations and plotted them on his map. They were bearing toward Echo Canyon along the freight road, both men vigilant. Dust rose swirling around their horses' hooves, then settled to powder the roadside brush.

"Looks like nobody back at Fort Bridger decided to light out after us," Old Billy remarked after searching their back trail yet again for dust puffs. "That's mighty wise of 'em, too. Them doughbellies don't even want to get into a shooting affray with Billy Williams."

"Don't underrate the Mormon soldiers," Fargo cautioned. "They took on the best of the Mexican lancers and mowed 'em down like hay."

"Oh, them sons of bitches can fight," his companion allowed. "But they ain't gonna get their pennies in a bunch over a gentile woman. If this Skye Fargo look-alike, or whatever the hell he is, drifts on out of the territory, yestiddy should be the end to it."

"I'm thinking he won't," Fargo opined. "The odds are too

damn long against some jasper not only looking like me, but being rigged out like me. This is a thought-out plan, and we've only seen the opening skirmish in a nasty campaign to come."

Billy, busy cleaning his teeth with a matchstick, shook his head. "You are one cheerful bastard, Fargo. I s'pose we're both going to die of the drizzling shits, too?"

Fargo grinned. "You want cheerful, move back east to the land of steady habits and open a store. Out here it's best to face the facts before they face you."

Billy grunted. "Brother, you're right as rain on that. But who could be behind this scheme—just one man or a gang? You got any enemies?"

At that last question, Fargo glanced over at Billy and thumbed his hat back. Both men started laughing so hard they had to grab their saddle horns.

"That's right," Billy said. "Have I lost my buttons? The women of the West love you, but plenty of the men would love to air you out. Me, I always try to kill my enemies so they won't come skulking after me."

"So do I. But you can't kill all their kin and close friends."

"It's like a damn furnace out here," Old Billy carped. "Wait until we start across the Salt. We'll be dried to jerky."

Fargo was riding with his head hanging along the right side of the Ovaro. He suddenly drew rein.

Old Billy watched him stare into a juniper thicket and pulled his carbine from its boot. "What's on the spit, Fargo?"

"Those wagon tracks we been following turn in there."

"So? They also come out again, see there? Headed for Echo Canyon."

Fargo knocked the rawhide riding thong off the hammer of his Colt. Then he swung down and tossed the reins forward to hold the Ovaro in place. "Damn, eagle eyes, don't you see the other set of tracks? A lone rider turned in here, too, and then rode out to the west."

"How's it any of our mix? We're drawing wages to scout, not track pilgrims."

Fargo pushed his hat back and performed a deep knee-bend, studying the tracks of the lone rider. "The rear offside shoe is loose—*that's* our mix."

"Shit, piss, and corruption," Billy swore. "My easy wages are slipping plumb away from me."

Fargo drew his Colt and led the way into the thicket.

"Christ on a mule!" Billy exclaimed. "Somebody sure left in a puffin' hurry. There sits a coffeepot and a damn good frying pan, and look at them plates scattered around. It's like a polecat scattered them in the middle of a meal."

"It was a polecat, all right." Fargo's face looked grim as he pointed at a tumble of small boulders. "There's why somebody cut loose in a hurry."

Old Billy stared at the tacky blood and curdles of brain sprayed on the rocks. Ants were crawling all over it. "A head shot. But no corpse. Looks like your dead ringer has returned."

They spotted the shallow, newly dug grave only about ten feet away. There was no marker. The two men piled stones on the mound of dirt to discourage predators.

"You sure it's the same man that bulled Ginny?" Old Billy pressed as they looked around the small clearing.

Fargo mulled that one. "Most horses put more pressure on the rear offside shoe than any other, so it's hardly uncommon to find one a little loose. I have to tighten mine all the time. So, no, I can't be sure."

"Them brains and blood—mayhap somebody just butchered out a small animal for their meal."

Fargo walked over to the pan and glanced into it. "Nah. It's some kind of hash or scrapple—I see potato and salt meat, nothing fresh-killed."

"Besides," Old Billy corrected himself, "if it was all hunky-dory, who would just waltz off and leave that fine pan and coffeepot? Hell, truck like that is gold this far west."

"You were right the first time, Billy. My dead ringer is back. And you notice it looks like he only killed one. If you took it in your head to rob pilgrims, would you kill just one?"

The veteran Indian fighter shook his white-streaked head. "It's plumb loco. You kill none or you kill the whole caboodle. Why leave a witness and risk facing the hemp committee?"

Fargo nodded. "At least one survivor was left to spread the word that Skye Fargo is on a rape-and-murder spree."

Old Billy loosed a low, slow whistle. "God's garters, Fargo, some snake-bit coyote is out to get you shot."

"I wonder." Fargo removed his hat and wiped his forehead on one sleeve. "If it's that simple, why not just plug me from ambush? This is good terrain for it."

"Hell, I can't read no sign on a murderer's breast. Could be he just wants somebody to do his dirty work. You ain't the easiest man in the world to kill, Fargo."

Fargo led the way back out onto the trail. "Billy, I calculate that a man riding at a canter can make Echo Canyon in about an hour—you agree?"

"Thereabouts. But not if he's scouting for line-station locations."

Fargo dismissed that with a wave of his hand. "The job will have to wait. If we don't put the kibosh on this killer, we stand to lose more than our job."

"Well, on that score, might be politic to give Echo Canyon the go-by. Old son, that hole has got killers packed in like maggots in cheese. Happens they've got word about Killer Fargo burning down a pilgrim, they'll powder-burn you before you get off your horse."

"I'm not going just yet. You are. Think they've got a mercantile there?"

"They did last time I rode through. It's just a big army tent, and the prices make the gold camps look reasonable."

Fargo fished a double eagle from his pocket. "Lay in some reach-me-downs for me. Pants, shirt, and get me a hat—white or gray, not black. And break out your shaving gear for me before you ride out."

Old Billy gaped as if Fargo had announced he was flying to the moon. "The Trailsman is gonna scrape off his whiskers and shuck his buckskins?"

"Ain't that a better idea than painting a target on my back?"

Old Billy thought about it and nodded. "I reckon it is, at that. Your beard and buckskins is how everybody describes you. But why not just avoid the place?"

"Because whoever survived this attack today is almost surely there, and I need to find out what happened. Besides, we need to sniff the wind and hear what people are saying."

"Say, what about the Ovaro?"

Fargo grinned. "You got you a new horse, chumley."

"Me! I'll be shot out from under my hat."

"Pee doodles. You don't look a damn thing like me, and a black-and-white pinto is as common as the coyote dun. Hell, I can close my eyes and I can't tell you the exact markings on my horse. A paint is a paint."

"Fargo, you hog reeve, that animal is a stallion."

"So are you, Indian fighter. Nobody is surprised to see a man of your leather riding an uncut horse."

That last bit of calculated flattery worked. Old Billy huffed out his chest. "That's right, ain't it? 'Sides, I always wanted to fork that horse and put the wind in my hair. Say, he won't buck me?"

"Nah. He's friendly once he knows a man's smell. You might as well ride him into the canyon this first trip. We'll be going back together, anyhow, so let people see you on him alone first."

Fargo stayed Old Billy's hand when he started to pull the saddle off his Appaloosa. "Don't bother. Neither one of us has a saddle worth noticing, and a horse fights a saddle that isn't curved to its own back. Just switch out the rifles—you don't need that brass-framed Henry drawing notice."

The Ovaro swung his head around when Billy tugged the Henry from its sheath, trying to nip him. "Fargo, this stallion has got larceny in his eyes. You're *sure* he ain't a man-killer?"

"Get to the sewing lodge, Gertrude. That horse is easy-natured. But *don't* sink spurs into him, or he'll chin the moon. Just control him with your knees. If you need to ride full-bore, thump him a bit with your boot heels."

"Easy-natured? Sounds like I'll be straddling dynamite."

Still muttering, Old Billy rummaged in a saddle pocket and removed a straight razor and a bar of shaving soap, handing them to Fargo. "I should be back well before sundown unless they shoot me for my boots in the canyon."

He stepped up into leather and gigged the Ovaro forward. Fargo led the Appaloosa back into the shade of the thicket. He scoured out the abandoned frying pan with a handful of leaves and poured water into it from his canteen. Fargo was about to lather his beard when something white caught the corner of one eye.

He glanced toward a nearby boulder and saw a folded piece of paper weighted down with a stone. With a queasy churning of digestive gears Fargo walked over and picked it up, unfolding it.

The five words goaded him with the force of pointed sticks:

The curtain's coming down, Fargo.

5

Fargo's first thought, after reading the mysterious message, was that the killer's sights might be notched on him right now. His second thought was that he would already be dead if that were the case.

And if this unknown enemy merely wanted him dead, why the elaborate plan to frame him? No, this was a malevolent plot to destroy his reputation and eventually get him shot down like a rabid dog—or hauled to the gallows. Whoever was behind it almost surely knew he was scouting for the proposed Pony Express, and they had waited until he reached the Utah Territory to spring the trap.

Why Utah?

Because, his racing mind answered his own question, under Mormon law lynchings were illegal and strictly punished, as was vigilante action. Criminals, even those bound for the gallows, served one to two years in prison as "penitents" to save their souls. And Mormon prisons meant backbreaking labor, cold stone floors for beds, and weevil-infested bread and stale water for nourishment. And unlike back east, bust-outs were unheard of.

Somebody, Fargo realized, bore him a grudge beyond all grudges. And so far at least one innocent person was dead, another raped and slashed up, in the sick quest for revenge. If he didn't bring this to a screeching whoa mighty damn quick, even a disguise wouldn't save him.

Fargo shaved, nicking himself numerous times because of his unfamiliarity with a razor. For good measure he pulled the curved skinning knife from Billy's saddle and hacked off handfuls of his hair, bringing it up around his ears.

Fargo felt his new-shorn face and frowned. "Christ, feels like a baby's ass," he muttered, considering his beloved beard one more casualty of the "deadly double" killer.

The horses had received rough treatment during this latest job, so he stripped the Appaloosa down to the neck leather and gave it a good rubdown and currying. After that he broke down and cleaned all of his weapons, even whetting his Arkansas toothpick on a flat stone.

As promised, Old Billy returned well before sunset with a parcel tied to the saddle.

At his first sight of Fargo the old Indian fighter started to draw his fancy sidearm. Then, his discolored face registering shock, he sputtered with laughter and almost slid from the saddle.

"Fargo, is that you? Hoss, you look like one a them whatcha-callits—a cherub! I'm embarrassed to cut a fart around you."

"I look different, don't I?"

"Different? I'll tell the world! You could be a preacher or mayhap one a them singers on a riverboat."

"Stick a sock in it," Fargo snapped as Old Billy lit down. "Let me see them duds you got me."

Old Billy assumed a look of exaggerated innocence. "Now remember, pard, Echo Canyon ain't exactly the Ladies' Mile. They only got one mercantile, and the offerings is mighty skimpy."

Fargo broke the string with his teeth and tore off the wrapping paper. He shook out a new shirt and stared, speechless: It was a bright canary yellow with gaudy blue piping down the front.

"Fella claimed it's all the rage back in the States," Old Billy reported, barely managing a straight face. "Mighty popular for cider parties and such."

Fargo loosed a string of curses. "You cantankerous son of a bitch! The whole point is *not* to draw attention to myself. This thing will make a blind man take notice. You did this on purpose."

Old Billy flung his arms wide. "Do you believe for one blessed minute that anybody on God's green earth would expect to find Skye Fargo in *that* war shirt?"

Fargo was still steamed, but it was a good point. "What about the trousers?"

"Sturdy corduroy."

Fargo shook them out, lips curling in disgust at the very idea of wearing store-bought clothing. "Christ, Billy, I can see they're way too small. The bottoms will barely reach my boots."

Old Billy shrugged, barely meeting his eye. "All they had, son. All they had."

"You're a damn liar. These look to be exactly your size, not mine."

"Now that's a libel on me. But so what if it's maybe true? You'll just be getting yourself killed soon, and hell, that corduroy wears good. Somebody oughter get the use of 'em."

Fargo gave up and started stripping out of his buckskins. "Did the Ovaro cause you any trouble in Echo Canyon?"

"A few men tossed some curious looks my way. But when they seen the ugly cuss riding him . . . it's just like you said. I saw a few other black-and-white pintos there."

"The killer could own one of them. See any other stallions?"

"Not so's you'd notice, but hell, I didn't crawl under 'em to see if they was cut. There's news, though. A woman driving a four-in-hand rode in before me. Young woman, I hear, and a looker. Says her husband was murdered on the freight road by you."

Fargo, busy wrestling with the button loops on the shirt, glanced up. "She still there?"

Old Billy nodded. "She's joined a small group of pilgrims at the north end of the canyon. Name's Louise Tipton. According to one old biddy I heard talking at the mercantile, she won't swear it was you."

"We have to talk to her," Fargo resolved as he struggled mightily to get the cords over his hips. "She might've noticed something Ginny Kreeger didn't."

"Speaking of noticing things," Old Billy said, breaking into a fit of sputtering laughter, "them cords fit you like them tights in the Romeo and Juliet days. The gals are gonna *notice* you just fine, Trailsman."

"Hey, where's my money?" Fargo demanded. "I gave you twenty dollars. These pathetic rags didn't cost near that much."

Old Billy glanced at his boots. "Now, I told you prices is high in the canyon."

Fargo gave a long, fuming sigh. "You damn liar. Billy, what the hell do you *do* with all the money you beg, borrow, and steal? You won't pay for a drink, you never go to the whores, and you leave a card game the moment you lose a dime."

"Don't push it, Fargo. It's none of your beeswax."

Fargo surrendered with a shrug and practiced walking in his skintight pants. "The name's not Fargo anymore, savvy? My name is Frank Scully, and you're Jim Lawson. We're both hunters by trade and we're headed out to the Sierra gold camps to hire out. Got all that?"

Old Billy nodded. "Them's the same summer names we used back in Kansas when we busted that smuggling ring."

"They were good luck then, and I'm hoping they will be now. Let's wait another half hour and then ride to Echo Canyon. I want to make sure it's dark before I arrive in this clown outfit."

Echo Canyon was small and deep with sheer vertical walls of striated rock. It provided easy access, on its west side, because of a brisk-flowing creek. A raging river aeons ago, it had carved out a path through the rock. The clean, cold water and shade trees had begun drawing pilgrims back in the 1840s.

With pilgrims, however, came merchants, gamblers, and owlhoots. With only the law of the gun to maintain order, bullyboys and professional gunmen holed up there, often on the dodge from Mormon law. Three of them—Butch Landry, Orrin Trapp, and Harlan Perry—had selected a campsite near the entrance to the canyon. Nobody rode in or out without their knowledge.

"Deets done it up good today," Landry told his companions as he poked at the fire with a stick to stir it up. "Killed some cooper named Mitt and then raped his wife."

"Now, see, that's the part I don't get," Orrin said. "I seen the woman when she rode in, and she's some pumpkins. You could hang a shelf on her tits. And here we are, *paying* Deets for gettin' under her petticoats."

Landry snorted. "Orrin, what's wrong with you and what doctor told you so? The quiff don't matter—it's getting the blame put on Fargo. And word's all over the canyon how Fargo done the dirty deeds. The woman named him."

Orrin's fox face looked even sharper in the dancing firelight. His eyes darted everywhere except toward the man he was speaking to. "To chew it fine, Butch, she named him but said she wasn't sure it was him."

"Hell, in a place like this that's good enough evidence. Won't nobody care about Mormon law—they'll cut him down the moment he shows up. We can't have that."

"Maybe he won't show up," suggested the third man, Harlan Perry. "We didn't find the son of a bitch all that predictable when he corralled us."

A long silence followed this truism.

"He'll show," Butch predicted confidently. "He made a point out of talking to the first woman Deets attacked, that Ginny somebody up at Fort Bridger. He'll want to palaver with this one, too."

"I don't know," Harlan said, shaking his head. "This plan of yours, Butch—it seems a mite too fancy."

"You wouldn't say that if Fargo killed *your* kid brother."

"Well, if you wanna see him suffer before he dies, we'll just strip him of his weapons and I'll beat the bastard into pudding."

The others knew this was no hollow boast. The huge Tennessean had once fought bare-fisted for the U.S Navy until he got drunk and beat a sailor to death for snoring. Perry preferred to beat his enemies rather than shoot them—beat them until they were crippled or dead.

"Harlan ain't no schoolmaster," Orrin put in, "but I think he's talking horse sense. Of course we need to plant Fargo and get revenge for Ralston. But this scheme of yours—it's eating up time we could spend pulling jobs. And I don't trust Deets—that fucker is tricky as a redheaded woman. Let's just ambush Fargo and shoot him to rag tatters."

Butch slowly shook his head. "You two just can't see it. You got no sense of what they call poetic justice."

One of the horses snuffled in the dark and Butch glanced that way quickly.

"Poetic justice?" Orrin repeated. "You wanna chew that a little finer?"

"Hearken and heed. Now, Skye Fargo ain't no scrubbed angel, right? He's a brawler and a womanizer, and he's got his name writ on the walls of plenty of frontier jails. But bone deep, he's a gentleman. One inkslinger called him a knight in buckskins. Serious crime ain't his gait. He'll look the other way when it comes to bootlegging or confidence games, but woe betide the murderer or rapist who crosses his path."

"All right," Orrin said, "so he's a crusader. What of it?"

"That's my point, chucklehead. If we just kill him the way you and Harlan want to, he dies a crusader. And out West legends grow taller than weeds. Doing it my way, we don't just kill Fargo—we kill the legend. And legends live a lot longer than men."

A column of sparks rose out of the fire, and all three men watched it.

"All that shines right to me," Harlan finally said. "Kill the legend with the man."

"I like it too," Orrin put in. "But I still don't trust Deets. That jasper ain't showing all his cards. You oughter left him back in Placerville."

"I think he's a weasel dick," Harlan agreed. "That son of a bitch would shoot a nun for her gold tooth."

"Deets is a one-man outfit," Butch conceded. "He's in it to win it—for himself. But as long as we keep his pocket full of rocks, he'll dance to our tune. Later, when Fargo is rotting in a Mormon prison and headed for a hanging, we'll solve the problem of Deets. We—"

"Shush it!" Orrin cut in. "Listen."

Above the soughing of wind and the brawling of water, they could hear hoof clops approaching along the solid rock bordering the creek. Riders were entering the canyon.

"Harlan," Butch said, his tone urgent. "Grab the pail and make like you're getting water. There's a full moon tonight;

you should get a good look at their faces. But just in case one of them is Fargo, don't give him a good look at you."

The big man hurried toward the creek. Along the opposite wall of the canyon perhaps a dozen big fires burned—the camp where the pilgrims had congregated to protect each other until they got out of Echo Canyon.

"Stupid sons of bitches," Butch said, spitting into the fire. "Thought they had it bad back in the States—rent was too high, jobs scarce, or maybe they got sick of scratching in the dirt for a few potatoes. Nobody told them about red savages, bone-dry deserts, rattlesnakes, or mountain fever."

"Or hombres like us," Orrin added.

Both men laughed. They knew that, out West, a man was just a face with a name. Nobody cared about his history—and nobody cared much about his future either. On the frontier few things were cheaper than a man's life.

"Speaking of pilgrims," Orrin said, "you heard any more about that Louise Tipton?"

"Nary a word. Yancy Johnson, that big Swede who shoes horses and mends harnesses, says she won't come out of her wagon. Don't seem likely Fargo will coax her out, if he's foolish enough to try."

"If he shows his face in this canyon by day, Butch," Orrin pointed out, "we'll never see him in prison *or* on a gallows."

"He knows that. Fargo's got a mind like a steel trap. Our job is to make sure he *doesn't* get killed here or anyplace else. It has to be Mormon soldiers or a Mormon posse that take him."

A shadow approached and then Harlan Perry's rawboned features were limned in the firelight.

"Well?" Butch demanded.

"Neither one of them was Fargo," Perry responded. "One was the stranger who rode in earlier today—about Orrin's size. He's riding a black-and-white pinto stallion, all right, but it ain't Fargo. Neither was the other one. He was shaved smooth with short hair and wearing a shirt that would make a horse blush. He's riding an Appaloosa."

Butch pondered all this. "The second man," he said, "wide shoulders?"

Harlan scratched his chin. "Reckon I didn't notice."

39

"Tall?"

"Now you mention it, he sat pretty high in the saddle."

Butch brooded over all this for a full minute. "I don't like it, boys. A pinto, all right. But a stallion? I say we best find out where these two put down for the night."

6

Both men stripped the horses and rubbed them down with burlap, then led them to the creek and let them tank up.

"Not much graze around here," Fargo remarked. "We'll have to grain them again tonight. Best put them on half rations—grain is low and we won't likely find more until Salt Lake City."

"What *ain't* in low supply is bedroll killers," Old Billy said. "You see that big oaf with the water pail when we rode in? That bastard glommed us good."

"I saw him, all right," Fargo replied. "And that ugly map of his looked familiar. But he turned away too quick."

Fargo had reluctantly cached his Henry and Arkansas toothpick in a clutch of rocks before riding into the canyon—while not uncommon weapons on the frontier, both were closely associated with him. It was dicey enough that Old Billy was riding the Ovaro.

The two men had picked an isolated spot with no fires burning nearby. The ground was rocky and hard with only a few scrub bushes to break the wind—the last campsite Fargo would pick under better circumstances.

"Them's the pilgrims over there," Old Billy said, rolling his head over his right shoulder toward the circle of fires. "The gal you need to talk to is in a big prairie schooner at the south end. I say you're a bigger fool than God made you if you go waltzing up to her and start asking questions. Fargo, this bunch don't care a jackstraw about Mormon law—the first hint of trouble and they'll shoot us to sieves."

"You're preaching to the choir," Fargo assured him as he did his best to soften up some bed ground with Billy's war hatchet. "I'd rather go talk to her at night when it's harder to make out my features. But the woman's just lost her husband, and the rest will be watching out for her. It'll have to wait for morning."

Old Billy snickered. "That's best anyhow. Your new duds will throw them off the scent. You look like—"

"I know what I look like, you jackass. But I'll grant you one thing—the last thing I look like is a killer."

Fargo paused as he unrolled his blanket. "Dammitall, Billy, that jasper with the water pail looked mighty familiar. His nose has been busted at least twice. I'd swear I know him from someplace."

"Fargo, you've tangled with half the hard cases in the West. Ain't no big shock happens a few of 'em are holed up here. Hell, the whole world knows that Mormons avoid this place—especially after the Mountain Meadows Massacre. So their soldiers hardly never come through here."

Fargo conceded the point in silence. He removed a handful of crumbled bark from a saddle pocket and set it ablaze with a phosphor, then piled on some sticks Old Billy had scrounged up. He poured water into a can, tossed in a handful of coffee beans, and set it in the fire to boil.

"Fargo," Old Billy said, "one thing's prickin' at me. This jackal who's raping and killing in your name—where is he holing up?"

"That's a stumper," Fargo admitted. "I been pondering it myself. If he actually does bear a strong resemblance to me, then he's as much a fugitive as I am."

"More," Old Billy pointed out. "He can't skin his beard off like you can or else he won't look like Fargo. Same with the buckskins and the black-and-white pinto."

"The way you say," Fargo agreed. "He needs all that to frame me. But what if, say, he's an actor? They're experts with disguises—so are confidence men. A beard can be glued in place with spirit gum, hair can be dyed in a hurry—you take my meaning."

"And if that's the gait," Old Billy said, "it's a real pisser. That means the son of a bitch could be in this canyon right now or any other high-old place he pleases. Hell, he could stand us to a drink and we wouldn't even know him."

"Hell, don't sugarcoat it," Fargo said sarcastically.

Old Billy cursed. "Fargo, you're nothing but trouble. Every time I start on a job with you for honest wages, it turns into shooting scrapes with sneaky, conniving sons of bitches who shoot from behind. At least an Indian warrior likes to count coup and look a man in the eye when he kills him."

"I didn't start all this, you lummox."

"I never said you did. But we got a job to finish, and how we s'posed to do it while we're huggin' with this killer?"

"Simmer down," Fargo told him. "On the way to the canyon I spotted our next line station—I just need to jot down the coordinates. Remember, this killer knows I'm following the Pony Express route, which makes his job easier. He's not going anywhere and neither are we."

Billy made a sputtering noise with his lips. "Well, as long as we make his goddamn job *easier*. Fargo, the Western sun has turned your brain soft. 'He's not going anywhere and neither are we.' You need to see a bumpologist, get your skull read."

A stick snapped, somewhere in the shadows on Fargo's left, and both men filled their hands, rolling to new positions.

"Please don't shoot me," called out a musical feminine voice. "Your coffee smells so good I just came over to beg a cup."

Fargo watched a pretty face, framed by blond coronet braids, materialize out of the darkness. Her body in no way lagged behind the face: A shimmering, emerald-green dress showed a well-filled bodice and an hourglass figure.

He rose up from the ground and slid his saddle in her direction. "It's not exactly a velvet wing chair, miss, but it's the best we can offer."

She hiked up her dress and plopped gracefully into the saddle, revealing two well-turned ankles. Billy used his hat as a potholder and poured her a cup of the steaming coffee. "Care for sugar, Miss . . .?"

"Reed. Caroline Reed. No, thank you, sir. I like my coffee bold."

Like my men, her tone seemed to add as she studied Fargo's ruggedly handsome face in the flickering flames.

"My name is Frank Scully," Fargo told her. "That's my partner, Jim Lawson."

"Pleased." She pursed her lips, blew on the hot coffee, and took a sip. "Oh, my, that is strong and good. We been out of coffee since west Texas."

"We?" Fargo said.

"Me, Uncle Ralph, and Aunt Esther. They've raised me since my folks was took by the cholera in 'forty-eight."

"And done a damn fine job of it," Billy opined, openly ogling the young woman.

"Thank you," she replied, completely unabashed.

"We're happy to have you," Fargo said, "but this isn't the safest place for a gal to go wandering around in at night."

She seemed transfixed by Fargo's face. "That's what Uncle Ralph says, too. But now and then I just get an itch to go . . . wandering. Our wagon has a busted axle and it's taking just forever to repair it. It gets so boresome of a night, and me not having a husband nor nothing."

Old Billy almost choked on his coffee.

"So, Frank," she said, "what do you and your partner do?"

"We're hunters."

She giggled. "In *that* shirt? It looks like the flag for some tiny nation in South America."

Fargo felt heat flood his face while Billy guffawed.

"It's like this, darlin'," Billy explained. "Far—I mean, Frank here runs off into the woods. When the game sees that shirt of his, they turn tail and run in my direction and I shoot 'em. 'Cept for them as tries to mate with him."

She giggled again. "I never did see such a handsome man wearing such foolish clothing. 'Course, it don't hide your wide shoulders none. Say . . . have you fellows heard what happened to Mrs. Tipton?"

"Who's Mrs. Tipton?" Fargo asked.

"Louise Tipton. Why, the poor thing! Pretty as four aces and left a widow this very day. Her husband, Mitt, was murdered out on the freight road. She's taking it mighty hard. She ain't said nothing, but some of the women say she was . . . outraged, if you take my meaning. Gal that fetching musta been."

"Damn shame," Fargo said. "They catch whoever did it?"

"Nuh-uh. But everybody's saying it was Skye Fargo."

"I can't place the name," Fargo said.

"Well, he's sort of famous. The Trailsman, they call him. Uncle Ralph says he's the best scout, tracker, and Indian fighter in the West."

"Best Indian fighter?" Old Billy cut in. "That don't cut no ice with me. Why—"

"Jim," Fargo cut in with a warning tone, "never interrupt a lady."

"Best Indian fighter my sweet aunt," Old Billy muttered, miffed.

"Did Mrs. Tipton name him?" Fargo asked the girl casually.

"Well, she did and she didn't. The man said he was Skye Fargo, and looked a lot like him. But she didn't seem so sure it was. Aunt Esther says she's still nerve-frazzled. Maybe by tomorrow she'll be able to make sense of it."

"Sounds to me," Old Billy remarked, sticking the knife into Fargo and giving it the "Spanish twist," "like this Skye Fargo is a mad dog off his leash."

"Uh-huh, and it surprises folks that know of him. This today wasn't the first attack. A rider come in from Fort Bridger and said Fargo attacked a young gal up there. Outraged her and cut her up real bad. Some of the men are whipped up into a frenzy—say they don't give a hang about Mormon law, they're gonna break every bone in his body and then drag-hang him slow."

"Even that's too good for the son of a bitch, you ask me," Old Billy said, watching Fargo with a sly grin on his face.

"Nobody did ask you," Fargo said in the same warning tone. "Sounds to me like folks need to wait and hear what Mrs. Tipton has to say. Mistaken identity is common out West."

"Uncle Ralph says the same thing," Caroline chirped. "Anyhow, it's lucky for her there's a real doctor in camp. He just rode in, and he's taking good care of her."

"A doctor?" Fargo repeated.

"Uh-huh. Dr. Jacoby. An elderly gent from Baltimore."

Obviously tired of all this gossip, she set her cup down and reached over to take Fargo's hand. "Would you like to take a walk, Frank? There's a real nice spot down the creek a ways. Nice soft grass—and real private. The stars are pretty tonight."

"I wouldn't mind stretching my legs," Fargo agreed, pushing to his feet with difficulty in the tight corduroys.

"You two take a care out there," Old Billy called out behind them. "This Fargo sounds like one dangerous son of a bitch."

Caroline tugged Fargo eagerly along in the direction of the fast-moving creek. They emerged from a clump of hawthorn bushes and spotted the water, gleaming silver in the moonlight.

"See?" she told him, indicating the ankle-deep grass all around them. "Makes for a soft carpet."

Fargo suspected that the ardent young woman had been here plenty already, but what did he care—right now it was *his* turn, and he hadn't topped a woman in more weeks than he cared to remember. He pulled her down beside him in the cool grass.

"Let me get this foolish shirt off," she murmured, starting to undo the button loops. "A man with a chest like yours— why, it's like covering a mahogany table with an oilcloth."

While she unfastened his clown shirt, Fargo reached behind her and undid the stays of her bodice, tugging it down. A pair of hefty, strawberry-tipped breasts gleamed like polished ivory in the moonlight. While he unbuckled his gun belt and set it aside, he moved back and forth between spearmint-tasting nipples, licking and nibbling them stiff.

"Land o'Goshen, Frank!" she gasped. "You seem to know what you're doing! My stars, that feels good—gets me all stirred up and warm down in my valentine."

She shucked his shirt off and gasped. Not only at the rock-hard pectorals and stomach, but at the startling array of bullet wounds, knife scars, and old burns.

"A hunter! What exactly do you hunt—or should I say who?"

"Honey, this is no time for my memoirs. You've got me all het up, and I'm ready to burst a seam here."

Fargo wasn't exaggerating. The ridiculously small and tight trousers Old Billy had bought him were especially constricting now that Fargo was fully aroused. While Caroline lay back and hiked her skirt up to her navel, Fargo struggled with the cords. Only with a massive final effort did he work them over his hips enough to free his straining length.

The moon wash was generous, and the slack-jawed woman stared at his raging manhood. "Sakes and saints! That lovely thing needs its own cage!"

"I agree," Fargo said, rolling on top of her and settling into the saddle. "Let's put him in one right now."

Fargo probed the pulsating dome in between the soft petals guarding her portal and shoved half his length into her tight, slick velvet tunnel. She shuddered and raised both legs, locking her ankles behind the small of his back.

"I feel filled up already," she gasped, "but pour the rest to me!"

Fargo flexed his buttocks and drove in her to the hilt, then began powering in and out like a steam drill, driving her to gasps and incoherent mutterings. It felt like ants biting his back as her fingernails dug into him, and soon the vigor of their coupling was moving both of them through the grass.

"Oh, Lord, Frank!" she cried out, "I'm gonna ex . . . *plode*!"

This horny lass didn't just come, she *arrived*. As she thrashed and groaned beneath him Fargo could hold back the floodgates no longer. In thrust after thrust he spent himself, collapsing on her like a rag doll.

For a full minute their muscles felt like jelly and their breathing was ragged and uneven.

"My stars," she finally whispered. "A man like you could make a gal an old maid for life."

"How so?" he replied, grimacing as he tried to get his "Romeo tights" back over his hips.

"Well, a stud as good as you ain't the marrying kind. But once a woman's had it with a man like you, she ain't likely to settle for these sixty-second wonders."

Fargo was about to reply when he heard a boot scuff somewhere in the darkness beyond the hawthorn bushes.

"Get dressed quick," he whispered in her ear, "then hie on back to your camp. We might have trouble here."

"Can I come see you tomorrow night?" she whispered back.

"Sure," he replied, doubting very much that he'd be here tomorrow night.

Fargo buckled on his gun belt while she fastened her bodice and disappeared along the creek. He crept forward, Colt in hand, stepping carefully. Before long he spotted a shadow dead ahead. The intruder seemed to be intently watching Old Billy as the latter sliced salt pork into a frying pan.

"Seen enough?" Fargo said behind him.

The man whirled with surprising agility, a gun muzzle spitting red orange flame. Fargo snapped off a return shot, and the man went crashing through the brush toward the mouth of Echo Canyon. But Fargo had carelessly forgotten something about Old Billy: The Indian fighter had survived all these decades through lightning-fast reflexes—and after dark he always broke out the heavy artillery.

"Jim!" Fargo shouted. "Don't—!"

But it was too late. Fargo dropped onto his face as if he'd been pole-axed just as the big Greener roared out, splitting the silence of the canyon.

7

Leaves and small branches were stripped just above Fargo as the load of lethal buckshot blew a tunnel through the foliage.

"Cease fire, you crazy son of a bitch!" Fargo boomed out. "It's me, Scully. The other shooter hightailed it."

"Well, God's blood, Far—Frank. Where you been? Bust your leg in a badger hole? At least *pretend* you got more brains than a rabbit. You know better than to approach an Indian fighter's camp at night without giving the hail."

Fargo broke into the circle of firelight, brushing himself off. "I didn't have time. Whoever was spying on you opened up on me."

Old Billy grunted. "Most likely bedroll killers looking to clean us out. This canyon's crawling with 'em."

"Could be," Fargo agreed, though a gut-hunch made him wonder.

"'Pears to me we best go turnabout on guard duty tonight," Old Billy suggested. "A dog likes to return to its own vomit."

"I s'pose, but if that yellow cur heard your Greener—and he had to—he won't likely sniff around here again."

Old Billy lowered his voice to just above a whisper. "Fargo, when it comes to the mazy waltz, your powder load ain't what it used to be. Used to was, when you slipped off into the brush with a comely lass, you *kept* her there awhile. Heaped your plate with seconds and thirds. S'matter, was this one poor fixin's?"

"Oh, she was a reg'lar banquet," Fargo said regretfully. "And I enjoyed the first course. But I had one of my God fears gnawing at my belly."

Old Billy, a great believer in signs, portents, and "tinglings," leaned forward with sudden interest. "Ahh? What was it, chumley? Goosebumps on your neck?"

"Well, first off, it was the woman Caroline. Now, she was right out of the top drawer. I've had pretty women make it easy before, but hell, she served it up on a platter."

Old Billy mulled that. Like Fargo, he avoided staring into the fire and ruining his night vision.

"You got a pint there. But a hussy is a hussy, and it's likely true she finds this place mighty boresome of a night. Never mind how you're dressed like a catamite, women always has been drawn to you."

Fargo swallowed the flattery without difficulty. "Yeah, she might be just what she seems—a young gal with the tormentin' itch. But that oaf we saw when we rode in, and then this jackal watching you—I got a hunch there's somebody in this canyon who's keeping their eyes peeled just for us."

"Happens that's so, then don't it seem likely they're in on these attacks that's being put on you?"

"The hand that whirls the water in the pool," Fargo replied, "stirs the quicksand."

"Then consarn it, Fargo, you're a bigger fool than God made you if you stay here."

Fargo thumbed a reload into the cylinder of his Colt. "Simmer down, stout lad. Just because they might be watching for us doesn't mean they know I'm here. Not yet, anyhow. We'll light a shuck out of here, all right, but I need to try to talk to Louise Tipton first."

Old Billy shook his head. "Why? She already said it was you what killed her man."

"Nah, that's not what Caroline told us. She said the man identified himself as Skye Fargo, but that Mrs. Tipton wasn't so sure. I need to find out *why* she wasn't so sure. That might be the clue I need to put handles on this masquerading bastard."

Old Billy let out a long, fluming sigh. "Mayhap you're right. We got damn little to go on—not even a hind tit. But you heard what else the girl said—how there's this Doc Jacoby hovering over the woman."

"Yeah," Fargo said softly, "ain't that convenient?"

Billy missed his tone. "Hell, you know how doctors is all

know-it-alls. Why would he let a drifter dressed like a whorehouse swamper talk to the Tipton woman?"

"That's one nut I haven't cracked yet," Fargo admitted. "It calls for wit and wile."

"Wit and wile," Old Billy groused. "This was a simple job when I hired on. Help you fight off the featherheads while you spotted good locations for line stations for the Pony. Russell, Majors and Waddell ain't patient men, Fargo. They still got to get all these stations built and hire men to run 'em. Happens we come in way behind schedule, that throws the whole shootin' match off."

"No need to fret," Fargo replied. "We're ahead of schedule already, and besides, I told you we're gonna keep on with the job. We just won't let on that's what we're doing or who we are. If a posse stops us, we're just hunters riding west to the goldfields."

Fargo brought the horses in even closer for the night, giving each of them a hatful of crushed barley. He stood first watch as the fire died down to embers and Old Billy snored with a sawmill racket. Fargo kept his Colt to hand and changed locations frequently, listening to the night. All was quiet, however, except for the snuffling of horses and the occasional drunken laugh from a distant campsite. Now and then something slithered in the brush, but Fargo's frontier-honed hearing could tell a snake or foraging animal from a human footfall.

Fargo was about to kick Old Billy awake when a gunshot erupted from the circle of wagons across the way, seeming especially loud in the late-night stillness.

Old Billy, who always slept on his weapons, sat up instantly. "Up and on the line, Fargo!" he called out, kneecaps popping as he came to his feet, Greener cradled in the crook of his left arm.

"Nix on that Fargo business," Fargo whispered. "The name is Frank Scully."

"Unh. The hell's going on?"

Normally Fargo would not worry overly much about a single gunshot in a place like Echo Canyon. With all the cheap 40-rod and Indian burner flowing in these places, one or two shots often signaled celebration and went ignored.

But this one was already more ominous—a hubbub of voices boiled up from the direction of the pilgrim camp, and figures carrying lanterns were all congregating on one prairie schooner.

"C'mon," he told Billy. "There's a game afoot, but stay back in the shadows. I got a hunch it's more bad news for Skye Fargo."

"And the stupid son of a bitch siding him," Old Billy muttered, falling in behind Fargo.

They joined the stream of curiosity seekers headed across the narrow canyon. A few persons carried lanterns or torches, and Fargo edged away from the wavering penumbra of light.

"Hell," Old Billy rasped in his ear, "they won't recognize you in this light—your hat throws your face in shadow anyhow."

"It's not my face I'm worried about—it's this damn shirt you bought. It's finally dawned on me that, seeing as how you bought it here, somebody else has seen it at the mercantile. And they might start wondering why the new stranger had to buy a shirt. Especially a puke rag like this."

"Anything I can do to get you killed," Billy shot back, grinning wickedly.

The two men pressed close to the knot of people outside the wagon. Fargo watched a tall, elderly man with a full white beard and a monocle step out onto the box holding a lantern.

"Ladies and gentlemen," he announced in a voice surprisingly strong and clear for his apparent age, "I have sad tidings to impart. Mrs. Louise Tipton has taken her own life by means of a pistol shot."

Outraged and shocked voices erupted. The man Fargo assumed was Dr. Jacoby raised his free hand to silence the crowd.

"In some measure," he continued with the crisp enunciation and voice projection that Fargo associated with stage actors, "I feel I am partly responsible for this tragedy. As many of you know, the late Louise Tipton was my patient. I was standing careful vigil over her, fearing just this contingency."

"The hell's a contingency?" Old Billy whispered. Fargo elbowed him silent.

"I searched the wagon for weapons," Jacoby continued, "and kept this poor, suffering creature in my constant view. But of course nature calls all of us, and as she appeared to be sound asleep after I gave her laudanum, I stepped off into the bushes for only a moment. She must have been feigning sleep, for it was then that she took the weapon from her skirts and ended her own life."

"Hell, it ain't your fault, Doc!" a voice rang out. "It was Skye Fargo done this! How do we even know it was suicide? They say Fargo can sneak up on a sleeping Indian and steal his medicine bag without waking him. Could be he killed her to shut her up!"

Another explosion of voices. Then a musical female voice Fargo recognized as Caroline Reed rang out.

"That's tarnal foolish! If Skye Fargo didn't want Mrs. Tipton to tell on him, he woulda killed her earlier when he killed her man. That would be a lot easier than doing it now."

Some in the crowd agreed with this. The hotheads, however, hissed and made catcalls.

"Besides," said a man close to Fargo, "I heard Louise Tipton when she first got to Echo Canyon. She said she wasn't sure it was Skye Fargo that done for her husband."

"I am no lawyer," Jacoby said. "The wound is consistent with suicide in that there are severe powder burns around her temple, proof the muzzle was close. And the gun is still clutched in her hand."

"That's just the same," a man chimed in, "as if she was killed at close range, ain't it? Hell, wouldn't take but a few seconds to plant the gun in her hand."

"All true," Jacoby conceded. "And the young lady was correct when she pointed out Fargo could have killed Mrs. Tipton earlier when he killed her husband. But as to the point about Mrs. Tipton saying she wasn't sure it was Fargo—that was mere shock and nervous agitation confusing her. I spoke to her at great length once she calmed down, and what she meant to say was wholly different. She *meant* that she couldn't believe a man of Fargo's reputation could do such a heinous thing. She never doubted who her attacker was."

It was as if Jacoby had lobbed a bomb. The crowd exploded with rage. The excited talk lasted for minutes.

Old Billy leaned close to Fargo again. "Contingency . . . heinous. Is that son of a bitch palavering in American or French?"

"Whatever the lingo," Fargo muttered back, "he's burying Skye Fargo with it."

A middle-aged matron stood on Fargo's right.

"Excuse me, ma'am," he said politely. "That Dr. Jacoby looks like a gent I once met in the Nebraska Territory. Is he a family man, do you know?"

"Confirmed bachelor," she replied, regret coloring her tone. "Several of the ladies have paid calls, but although he's gallant, he's apparently married to his calling."

"This gent I'm thinking of rode a big roan gelding. Is that still his horse?"

The woman gave Fargo a startled glance in the flickering light, especially his ridiculous shirt. In 1850s America genteel women did not discuss livestock, or mention words like "bull" or "gelding." Fargo realized his mistake too late.

"I beg your pardon, madam," he hastily added. "I've been back of beyond so long that my parlor manners have rusted."

This made Old Billy snort. The matron, however, found Fargo's apology acceptable. "Now that you mention it, young man," she replied, "I've never seen Dr. Jacoby mounted—always on foot. Of course, the canyon is small."

"It is," Fargo agreed, grabbing Old Billy by one elbow and guiding him back toward their camp.

"At first light," Fargo told him, "we're putting this place behind us."

"Well, strike a light! I never wanted to come in the first place."

"Oh, it was worth it," Fargo assured him. "I'd say that Dr. Jacoby, whoever the hell he really is, is our killer."

Old Billy stopped in his tracks, watching Fargo in the moonlight as if he had just announced he was the Queen of England. "Fargo, are you touched? That old man, raping and killing? Hell, his fires are banked by now. And outside of being tall, he don't look one thing like you."

"Does your mother know you're out? He's younger than

you. The man's an expert at disguises—maybe a stage actor judging from the way he worked that crowd with his voice—a young, strong voice."

Old Billy mulled this. "He *did* seem awful spry when he hopped up on that box. Yeah . . . and his voice—say! And the doctor business—"

"Was a ruse to get him close to Louise Tipton. See, even more than Ginny Kreeger up at Fort Bridger, Louise didn't buy the whole bill of goods. When he realized that, he had to kill her—stone her into silence, as the Comanches put it."

"Well, it all fits," Old Billy said, "but it's a passel of conclusions to make without more evidence."

Fargo nodded. "There's also his horse. That woman just now told me she's never seen him on it. Could be because it's a pinto stallion and hidden somewhere."

"But why's he doing all this? Sure, he's put the no-good label on you, but he's running a helluva risk, too."

"My guess is he's just a paid jobber. Someone else has put him up to it. He's got to have support."

"I take your drift," Old Billy said. "Mayhap that was no bedroll killer we fired at tonight."

"Yeah, and there was that galoot watching us when we rode in."

"But it just don't cipher," Old Billy complained as they reached their camp. "It's easier to blow up a mountain than to tunnel through it. Why not just kill you and get it over with?"

"I've been over this trail already. Whoever this is doesn't want to just kill me—he wants to kill my reputation first. That's my best guess anyhow."

Fargo shucked out his Colt and walked a quick circle around the camp. Leaving his boots and gun belt on, he crawled into his blankets. "It's your watch, old son. Remember—these heel flies might decide to change their plan and just kill me outright. Keep your eyes peeled."

"If it's only you they mean to kill," Old Billy replied, "it's no skin off my ass."

Butch Landry, Harlan Perry, and Orrin Trapp had been among the crowd when Dr. Jacoby spoke. They returned to their camp before they discussed the matter.

"You boys think the Tipton woman really done herself in?" Perry asked.

Butch and Orrin exchanged an incredulous look.

"Harlan, have you been grazing locoweed?" Butch replied.

"Well, hell, that doctor said—"

Butch and Orrin burst into derisive laughter.

"Harlan," Butch said, "I like you. You're a big, strong son of a bitch, and you take orders good. But you musta been mule-kicked when you was a tad. That wasn't no goddamn doctor—it was Deets."

Even in the pale splashes of moonlight it was clear when Perry's eyes bulged out like wet, white marbles. "It was? No shit?"

"Why, hell yes. It ain't no problem for a trained actor like him to make himself look older."

"But I figured . . . I mean, Deets made a heap of doin's out of saying none of us could meet with him when there's folks around. When did he tell you?"

Now Orrin, still shaking his head, pitched into the game. "Harlan, we ain't met with him, you simp. It's all what they call deduction. Now this woman, this Louise Tipton—she drives into the canyon, looking like death warmed over, and claims a man calling hisself Skye Fargo murdered her man in cold blood. Now, do you believe it was Fargo that done it?"

"'Course not," Harlan shot back. "I ain't so clever as you two, but I ain't *that* stupid."

"All right," Orrin went on, his foxlike features clearer now that Butch had stirred up the embers, "the woman never said she *believed* it was Fargo—only that the killer said he was. Now Deets had already followed her in to see what kind of story she would tell. And when he heard what it was, he knew something had to be done in a puffin' hurry. The doctor disguise was perfect."

"Yeah," Harlan said, "now I see how the wind sets. He killed her and called it suicide."

"Not quite," Butch chimed in. He crimped a paper and shook some tobacco into it. "He said 'apparent' suicide or some such. When some in the crowd said Fargo snuck in to kill her, he never put the nix on that idea. He played his hand real slick. That's two deaths put on Fargo—two *murders*—and the rape and slashing of a gal up at Fort Bridger. That should be plenty to put the Mormon soldiers on his trail."

"Maybe," Orrin said, "and maybe not. I read in a Carson City newspaper how Fargo is popular with the Mormons. Once, there was a plague of locusts destroying all the crops around Salt Lake City. By sheer happenstance, just as Fargo reached the south shore of the lake, thousands of seagulls flew up from the lake and devoured the locusts. Fargo admitted it was just coincidence, but the Mormons took it as a sign."

Butch dismissed this with a wave of his hand. "Such claptrap won't stand up to politics. Don't forget, the U.S. government has been trying for years to stop these wivin' Mormons from having their harems. Brigham Young has told his people not to ruffle any gentile feathers. Arresting and convicting a notorious murderer and rapist of gentiles will be a goodwill gesture."

"That's likely," Orrin agreed. "But you heard that crowd a little while ago. They ain't got arrests and trials on their minds."

Butch nodded. "'Pears like Deets has done his job *too* good. Boys, all you can do with an avalanche is get out of its way. We might not be able to pull off my original plan. We just might have to settle for seeing Fargo beaten and lynched. But we won't toss in our hand just yet—if we can steer the Mormons on to Fargo, or him on to them, before the rabble get him, it's prison *and* the gallows."

"It's all one to me," Orrin said. "But while Deets is out there painting the landscape red with blood, we got to somehow keep better track of the real Fargo."

"Amen and hallelujah," Butch said. "But he's a hard man to close herd. That's where I think we maybe got lucky—I think those two hardcases who rode in tonight are Fargo and that Indian fighter siding him."

"Why here?" Orrin asked.

"To talk to Louise Tipton."

"Hell, he shouldn't even have known about her yet."

Butch exhaled a long sigh. "Orrin, are you as slow as Harlan? Skye Fargo has been reading sign all his life—and not just trail sign. Likely, he rode right onto the spot where Deets plugged her old man. I wish we could get a closer look at their horses—especially the saddlebags."

"I ain't going near that camp again," Harlan vowed. "One a them parted my hair with a sidearm while the other lit me up with a scattergun. I still got a few pellets in my ass, and they burn like bee stings."

"Don't fret," Butch said, "no more poking fire with a sword. But the homely one riding the black-and-white pinto—Orrin, have you ever seen a likeness of this Billy Williams the crap sheets have mentioned?"

"Can't say as I have. He ain't famous like Fargo, but I've heard his name mentioned a few times. They say he's a specialist in depopulating Indians."

"I wonder," Butch mused aloud, "if he just switched horses with Fargo."

"Deets would know," Orrin said. "He's spied on the two of them from a distance."

"Yeah, but we won't be palavering with him until Fargo passes Salt Lake City."

Orrin settled into his bedroll. "You mean *if* he passes Salt Lake City. From what I heard tonight, Fargo might be damn lucky to get out of Echo Canyon."

"That double-rough bastard has pulled his tail out of tighter cracks than this place," Butch reminded his comrades. "But is he even *here*? If he ain't, then I want to know where the hell he is. You know—keep your enemy close and all that."

"Then we'll have to talk to Deets before Salt Lake City," Orrin said. "He's the only one might know."

"That ain't such a good plan," Harlan spoke up. "'Member when we hired him on out in Placerville? He said it was im—im—"

"Imperative," Butch supplied impatiently.

"Yeah. Imperative that we don't meet with him on account of us being wanted men."

"That's claptrap," Butch said. "*He's* riding the owlhoot trail himself. I didn't tell you boys this, but I will now. I saw it on a wanted dodger in Carson City—before he started working confidence games in the Sierra gold camps, Deets was a hack actor in San Francisco. But he raped and killed a popular actress named Belle Lajeunesse. According to the dodger, she 'spurned his advances' and he got blood in his eye."

Orrin sat up and whistled. "An actor. So that explains how come he's so good with disguises. And that's why we found a man that smart rooking prospectors for chump change."

"Yeah, but lissenup," Butch cautioned. "Both of you, hear? We don't know jack shit about him being an owlhoot. Don't bring it up to him—they don't just hang a man in San Francisco, not for killing a popular female. That place is run by the Hounds, that vigilante bunch from the Barbary Coast. They'll break every bone in his body and then pack gunpowder in his nostrils and light it. If Deets finds out we know, he'll run like a river when the snow melts."

Butch fell silent for a moment and brooded as he gazed into the fire.

"Orrin's right," he decided. "Deets will be dusting his hocks out of here tomorrow morning. I know a safe place where we can waylay him and find out about these two new men. Damn it, pards, I got a hunch them two are Skye Fargo and Old Billy Williams."

8

At the first pale glimmer of dawn, Fargo and Old Billy ate a quick meal of cold pone and even colder creek water. They led their horses to drink, then tacked them and inspected their hooves and pasterns for cracks.

"Inspect all your weapons," Fargo said before they swung up into leather. "After that show 'Doc Jacoby' put on last night, we could be riding into a lead bath."

Old Billy hefted his big Greener. "Me and Patsy Plumb here are a mite fond of killing, Trailsman. I wasn't Bible raised, y'know."

Fargo grinned. "I got no squabble with the Good Book, but heathens like you are the only men I'll hire. But stay your hand on the killing unless we're forced to it. I generally prefer—"

"Wit and wile," Billy finished for him. "Crissakes, I'd figure you for a Quaker if I didn't happen to know you've left a trail of corpses from St. Joe to San Francisco. Fargo, you're the undertaker's best friend."

Fargo gripped the horn and stepped up and over, mounting the Appaloosa. "The name is Frank Scully. Far as the corpses, wit and wile has its limitations. And I've never yet killed a man who didn't require killing."

Old Billy forked the Ovaro and took up the reins. "Require? Oh, I've killed a few just to keep my hand in. Mostly when I was a younger buck. A few of 'em was outright murder, I reckon. That's why I don't cotton to the Bible—by Christian reckoning, I'm bound for hell."

Fargo gigged the Appaloosa toward the canyon entrance. "Oh, if there's a hell, likely we'll both fry everlasting. I try not to dally with married women, but officers' wives do get mighty lonely of a winter night."

Fargo fell silent, listening carefully to the canyon. The creek brawled noisily, and the dawn chorus of birds raised an unbroken music. Because of Echo Canyon's depth and steep granite walls, sunlight would not reach the canyon floor for hours. But there was enough daylight filtering in now to show shapes and muted colors.

Old Billy gigged the Ovaro up beside him. "See anybody stirring their stumps?"

"Just a couple men rustling up breakfast. Looks pretty peaceful. Maybe we'll roll a seven and ride out without trouble."

Instead, Fargo realized minutes later, they had rolled snake eyes. Three seedy-looking men armed with rifles blocked the only entrance to the canyon.

"Let's just kill 'em," Old Billy urged in a whisper. "We could do it faster than a finger snap."

"The killing would be easy," Fargo whispered back. "But that'll put the whole canyon on our spoor. Hold off for now."

The two riders reined in.

"Well," Fargo greeted them, "this looks like a grim situation."

"Nobody asked for your lip," said a heavyset, wreath-bearded man holding a Volcanic rifle aimed at Fargo. "What's your name, mister?"

"Frank Scully. This here's my partner, Jim Lawson."

"Uh-huh. You two rode in only last night, now you're making tracks. How's come the short stay?"

"Are you men duly sworn lawmen," Fargo came back, "or just self-elected regulators?"

A tall man with a lantern jaw wagged the barrel of his North & Savage magazine rifle. "You been warned about the lip, mister. We're all the law that's required to kill you."

Fargo saw Billy's right hand inching toward the Greener in his scabbard. "Nix on that, Jim," he muttered.

"What?" Wreath Beard demanded. "Speak up like you own a pair. How's come the short stay?"

"All we needed was water," Fargo replied. "This creek is the best water in this corner of Utah Territory. Our horses tanked up good and we filled our goatskins. But now we got to get out to California and find work."

"What kind of work?"

"We're hunters," Fargo said. "We hire out to the army, railroad crews, prospectors."

"Uh-huh." Wreath Beard studied the Ovaro. "You, purple face—where'd you get that stallion?"

"Your wife give him to me last time I fucked her. Told me a stallion deserves a stallion."

All three men were so shocked by this reply that they stood still as stone statues, jaws slack with surprise. Then Lantern Jaw sniggered.

Wreath Beard wasn't so amused. He swung his muzzle from Fargo to Old Billy. "Damn lucky for you, mouthpiece, that I ain't hitched. I asked you where you got that stallion. Now you best answer up or I'll kill you where you sit."

"It belonged to a Crow Indian up near Powder River," Billy spat out. "I killed the red son and kept his horse. Case you don't know it, Injuns never cut their horses."

"Hell, my grammaw knows that."

"Then it ain't no big freak, is it, to see a white man riding a stallion?"

"'Cept that this one," put in Lantern Jaw, "fits the exact description of Skye Fargo's hoss."

Fargo laughed. "Is that what this roadblock is all about— Skye Fargo? Then you gents need to study up—it's common knowledge that Fargo's Ovaro is trained to buck off any rider except him. That's how come his horse has never been stolen."

This was pure hogwash but Fargo doubted these flea-bitten rubes would know that. Wreath Beard turned to the third man, a skinny little runt with a pockmarked face. "Harney, you're the one reads up on Fargo. That true about his horse?"

Harney rubbed his chin, mulling it. "I don't rightly recall. It *could* be true. It sounds like something Fargo would do. His pinto is highly prized."

The three men stepped back a few paces and conferred quietly. They stepped forward again.

"You, Scully," Wreath Beard said to Fargo. "You claim as how you're a hunter. But you're armed with a carbine. A hunter uses a long rifle like a Henry. How can you bring down game with such a short barrel?"

"This Spencer is accurate out to two hundred yards. I drop

most of my game well under that. And the .56 caliber slug is a helluva knockdown bullet."

"You know, with a square-cut beard you'd look just like Fargo. Everybody knows he's a dead shot with the Henry. Let's see can you shoot that Spencer like you claim."

Wreath Beard searched the sky until he spotted a red-tailed hawk swooping in circles over the canyon. "Bring down that hawk, Scully."

Old Billy exploded. "The hell you want, egg in your beer? Scully don't shoot targets that small—he pops over deer and antelope and such. 'Sides, that hawk is priddy near three-hunnert yards off."

"Stow it, stain face. He claims to be a hunter that uses a carbine. Here's his chance to prove it."

Fargo shrugged and slid the Spencer from the scabbard of Old Billy's saddle. In fact he had fired a Spencer before in skirmishes with Indians, but this seemed an impossible shot—such a small target in motion would be difficult even with his Henry at this range.

Fargo levered a round into the chamber, settled the butt-plate into his shoulder socket and took up the trigger slack in a slow pull. He dropped the notch sight square on the bird, then edged slightly to the right to lead it. The gun bucked into his shoulder, a few feathers went floating off, and the hawk plummeted straight to the ground.

"By the Lord Harry!" Lantern Jaw exclaimed.

Wreath Beard looked astounded. He turned to the third man, evidently the resident scholar on the subject of Skye Fargo. "Harney, could Fargo ever make that shot with a carbine?"

"Are you loco? He couldn't make it with his Henry."

All three men lowered their muzzles. "All right, boys," Wreath Beard said. "You're free to go. Good hunting in California."

Both men followed the creek up to the high ground. With Old Billy watching their back trail, Fargo retrieved his rifle and knife from the rock cache.

"You know, Fargo," Old Billy finally said, "that shot you made just now will become back-country lore. I never seen the like."

"It was some pumpkins," Fargo admitted. "But truth to tell, it was luck. I couldn't do it again in a hundred years."

"Mebbe, but you're on to something with that wit and wile business. That was a stroke of genius when you told that stretcher about how the Ovaro would buck any rider but you. That got 'em to doubting."

"It was only partly a stretcher."

Billy frowned. "Well here I am, sittin' on his back like the King of Persia on his throne."

Fargo inserted two fingers into his mouth and loosed a piercing whistle. Instantly, the Ovaro jackknifed and Old Billy sailed off into the dust of the trail, landing in an ungainly heap.

Fargo laughed so hard he had to squat on his heels. Old Billy loosed a string of vile curses that would have been outlawed in hell. But Fargo's laughter was contagious and soon both men were wracked by spasms of mirth.

"Fargo," Old Billy finally said as he climbed to his feet, "life around you never gets tedious—you break out a new surprise every day."

Billy mounted the Ovaro and added, "Leastways you better or both of us will soon be carrion bait."

A mile west of Echo Canyon a huge tumble of boulders rose on the left side of the freight road. It was behind this excellent cover that Butch Landry's gang waited impatiently for James "Deets" Gramlich. He finally rode by around midmorning on his fine-looking pinto stallion.

"Deets!" Butch called out.

The man who had recently pawned himself off as Dr. Jacoby reacted with the reflexes of a man half his apparent age. In a mere heartbeat he produced a Colt revolver from beneath his frock coat.

"Leather that shooter," Butch said. "It's me, Butch Landry. Ride behind the boulders and hobble your pinto."

"I told you we'd rendezvous outside Salt Lake City."

"Yeah, but we'll make this worth your while. Won't take but a few minutes."

"Only gold will make it worth my while."

"I ain't talking about goober peas."

Gramlich reined off the trail and swung down, hobbling his horse foreleg to rear.

"So what is it?" he demanded, glancing at all three men in turn. "You're steamed, right, because Fargo is still on the loose?"

"Steamed?" Butch repeated. "In a pig's ass! You're doing great work, Deets. Won't be long before Skye Fargo is rotting in a Mormon prison."

"But how's come," Orrin put in, "you're still disguised like Doc Jacoby?"

"Yeah," said Harlan, "ain't you s'posed to be Fargo now?"

Gramlich snorted and shook his head as if to suggest that such stupidity ought to be bottled. "Use your noodles. Fargo has become the most wanted man in the Utah Territory. If I disguise myself as him all the time, I'll be gone beaver. It didn't matter when I first started, but now I have to save the Fargo disguise just for committing new crimes."

"Hell, that shines," Butch said. "See, what we wondered—"

"Plank your gold first," Gramlich cut in, extending his right hand. "We didn't agree on extra meetings. I'm taking a mountain of risks for you gentlemen."

Butch reached into a possibles bag on his belt and produced a chamois pouch, handing it over. "This oughter balance the ledger."

Gramlich opened the pouch and spilled five double-eagle gold pieces into his palm. He loosed an appreciative whistle. "Liberty heads! One hundred dollars worth. It's true, isn't it, Butch? Fargo rounded you three up and even killed your brother, but they never got the payroll gold."

"You keep your secrets," Butch said, "and we'll keep ours. What I—"

Harlan cut in. "Mr. Gramlich, how do you make that white beard stick to your face?"

"Spirit gum. For making my hair white I use axle grease and powdered alum. When I'm Fargo I have to dye it. My saddlebags are stuffed full of beards and wigs and such—I can even make myself into a woman."

Harlan looked fascinated and opened his mouth to ask more questions. But Butch feared the big, slow-witted man might mention Deets' past as an actor.

"Never mind, Harlan," Butch snapped. "Deets ain't here to set up school. What I'm wondering is if you noticed them two riders that come in after dark last night. Right off I suspicioned that they was Fargo and that Indian fighter, Old Billy Williams."

This announcement made Gramlich start, his face going almost as pale as his beard. "Fargo? In Echo Canyon?"

"I ain't certain-sure, mind you. If it's him, he shaved his beard off."

"Christ! If it was Fargo, he must have come to talk with the Tipton woman. That's what he did up at Fort Bridger with the young girl."

"Yeah, but you foxed him this time," Orrin said. "A man can't get much information from a corpse."

"If I killed her in time," Gramlich fretted. "Butch, did you see Fargo's horse?"

"I think so, but his pard was riding it. Fargo had him a white Appaloosa—"

"Shit!" Gramlich cut in. "That was Fargo, all right. He switched mounts with Old Billy. But how in Sam Hill did they get past those three regulators this morning?"

"Fargo could bamboozle the devil in hell. For some reason the regulators made him take a shot at a hawk circling a couple hunnert yards over the canyon. He dropped that son of a bitch plumb using a Spencer carbine."

"He didn't use his Henry?"

Butch shook his head. "Didn't have it with him—nor the Arkansas toothpick he carries in his boot."

Gramlich tugged at his fake beard. "Must've hidden them. Jesus Christ and various saints! I spent the night in the same canyon he did."

"Why does that boil your guts?" Orrin asked. "Ain't it better to know where he is?"

"If I know where he is, there's a rotten chance he knows where I am."

"Well he don't," Butch said, "or you'd a woke up dead this morning."

Gramlich stuffed the gold in his pocket. "You three aren't exactly safe as sassafras, either. Fargo is well informed for a man who inhabits the back forty, and I'd guess he knows by now that you busted out of prison."

"That's one reason for this meeting," Butch said. "You've done slick work, Deets, but trying to catch Fargo is like trying to nail smoke to the wall. Thanks to you every swinging dick in Utah is after him. But the manhunt has to grow wider, and fast, before Fargo notches his sights on us. That means pulling in the Mormon soldiers—every last one of them."

"You mean I should attack a Mormon girl, right?"

Butch nodded. "You do it all disguised as Fargo. So far it's mostly gentiles that are riled up on account you only killed outsiders. We need to get old Brigham himself so pissed off that he climbs off them nineteen wives of his and puts out the order to arrest the Trailsman."

"You favor that plan," Gramlich countered, "because you're obsessed with making sure Fargo gets arrested, imprisoned for a couple years, and then hanged. It's revenge for your brother, and I don't begrudge you that. But there comes a point where every gambler has to cut his losses—it might be wiser if the four of us teamed up to kill Fargo."

Butch stubbornly shook his head. "He'll be in Salt Lake City inside of two, three days. You can ride faster on account you ain't plotting out line stations for the Pony. Once you jump that Mormon—a young gal, and rape and slice her—Skye Fargo has reached the end of his trail. And you collect the balance of your gold."

Gramlich mulled all this for a full minute. "It just might be the best plan, at that. Mormons have a persecution mindset, and a crime like that by an outlander would rile the hive. Fargo can dupe ragtag vigilantes, but Mormon soldiers are no boys to mess with. All right, one more attack and this time it'll be a sockdolager."

9

The day was hot, the air so funereally still that it seemed to ring. Overhead, vultures wheeled like merchants of death, ever vigilant. Following the predetermined route of the soon-to-be-launched Pony Express, Skye Fargo and Old Billy bore southwest toward Salt Lake City.

Old Billy slewed around in the saddle so often to check their back trail that it finally got on Fargo's nerves.

"Damn it, old son, will you quit craning your neck like a nervous bird? A veteran Indian fighter like you needn't be so skittish."

"It ain't Indians what got me nerve-frazzled," Billy shot back. "It's hemp committees. Crissakes, you was in Echo Canyon when that Tipton woman done herself in. You heard that rabble talking up what they got planned for you. And since me and you is joined at the hip these days, ain't too likely they mean to feed me and send me on my way."

"Oh, sure as cats fighting they plan to kill you too," Fargo said cheerfully. "You're riding my horse, ain't you? And you gave me yours. That's what the Philadelphia lawyers call complicity. Yessir, William, you'll swing in the breeze right alongside me."

Old Billy scowled and made a fist. "I'll sink you, son. Sink you six feet closer to hell." He spat, just missing the Ovaro's ear.

Fargo grinned. "You best adjust that aim, Billy. If that nasty shit hits him, you'll be breathing cloud."

"He's better-natured than you, Trailsman. Least he don't make no jokes about his friends swinging in the breeze."

"You need to go to school, Old Billy. First of all, like I told you last night, Louise Tipton didn't kill herself. That graveyard rat Dr. Jacoby—who *ain't* no damn doctor—killed her. He's the same son of a bitch who killed her husband. She was s'posed to ride in hollering how Skye Fargo done for her man. But she upset the applecart when she started saying how she wasn't sure it was me."

"Fargo, when it comes to evidence to prove all that, you ain't got spider leavings. But all right, you got a good think-piece on you, you've gone wide upon the world like me, and just mebbe you're right. Could be that Jacoby is who you say he is. But so damn what? Them ignunt pilgrims don't give a frog's fat ass what the facts is—they been reading penny dreadfuls and they're all het up to throw a necktie party."

Fargo pulled down his hat against the swirling grit and glaring sun, then shrugged one shoulder. "Like you just said, so damn what? Do you really believe that a bunch of clabber-lipped greenhorns who don't know gee from haw are going to run *us* to ground? The Trailsman and the best damn Indian fighter since Dan'l Boone?"

Old Billy huffed out his chest. "Well, when you put 'er that way, not by a jugful. Say, them white-livered sons of bitches couldn't locate their own asses at high noon in a hall of mirrors."

Fargo laughed. "That's the gait. This is the third day now since Ginny Kreeger was attacked at Fort Bridger, and for all their bluster in camp, where's the regulators?"

He indicated the vast, sprawling land around them with an extended arm. The harshest terrain of all, the formidable Salt Desert, would not begin until west of Salt Lake City. But the land around them was sere and rugged: sterile mountains on the horizons and, closer at hand, a few gullies washed red with eroded soil, low, windswept mesas, and tall red-granite spires. The only growth in sight was scraggly saltbush and the ubiquitous sagebrush, which looked purple or gray depending on the light.

"This is damn close to being on the Great Plains," Fargo said, "when it comes to thwarting ambushes. Hell, a sparrow couldn't sneak up on us. So a lynch mob is shit out of luck. But let's not bamboozle ourselves, Old Billy. We still got two dangers."

"And one of 'em," his companion replied, "is Injuns. That's where you hired me to help."

Fargo nodded. "These animals we're riding can outrun any gaggle of pilgrims. And my Ovaro, depending on his condition, can outrun Indian mustangs. But the tribes out here slit their horses' nostrils for more wind, and they ride light compared to a white man's rigged mount. Your Appaloosa is a fine horse and I admire to be riding him. But he'll founder, won't he, in a run-down with Indians?"

Old Billy nodded. "I've rid to safety over short hauls. But in the Utah Territory it's stand pat or lose your dander. Still, I got me a few tricks when Red John is after my topknot. But what's that second danger you just mentioned?"

"Mormon soldiers," Fargo said bluntly. "They cap the climax. They're the best cavalry troops in the country. All their set-tos with Indians have made them masters of the long chase. They work in relays so even the Ovaro can't outrun them. Just like the Texas Rangers, they always get their man."

Old Billy nodded. "That's why I never run afoul of 'em. You really b'lieve they'd start a manhunt for a gentile attacking other gentiles? Most especial, when they're fighting mountain Utes in the Wasatch?"

Fargo shrugged. "Maybe, maybe not. But I'll bet you a plugged peso they'd form up to catch a gentile raping and killing a *Mormon* girl."

Billy started visibly. "A Mor—but that ain't happened."

"Yet, you mean. But look where we're headed—the capital of Deseret, Salt Lake City. This Fargo look-alike hasn't managed to get me hanged from a branch yet. Once we pass Salt Lake and hit the desert, he won't have much chance to frame me again. This could be his last shot, and he might decide to make it a good one."

Old Billy rubbed his chin, pondering it. "Damn you, Fargo, you always was good at thinking like a criminal. I fear you're right."

"So I'm gonna say it again—this might be a good time for you to cut and run. If we get Mormon soldiers salting our tails, it'll be curtains for both of us."

"That's just tough titty. I don't care a hoot in hell what

happens to your lanky ass. But I don't draw most of my pay until we pick that last line station near Sacramento."

Fargo glanced across at the stubborn old frontiersman. "You value the pay over your life?"

"Why, hell yes. I don't give a hang about one damn thing *but* money. I'd steal the coppers from a dead man's eyes. If they passed a law saying it costs every man one dollar to keep his pizzle, I'd learn how to squat to piss."

Fargo's smooth-shaven face became a mask of amazement. "Old son, you make King Midas look like a spend-thrift. Either you've got thousands stashed away by now or somebody is blackmailing you. What's all this mystery about you and money?"

Old Billy waved him off without comment.

Fargo gave up and stretched across to his own saddle, pulling out his U.S. Army field glasses. Slowly, methodically, he made a minute search in all four directions, looking for movement, not shapes. Then he reined in.

"Trouble?" Billy demanded.

"I can't say yet. There's dust puffs way to the north, but it could just be wind picking up."

Fargo lowered the glasses and watched the sweep of dark clouds way to the north. "Storm making up in that direction," he remarked.

However, Fargo hadn't survived on the frontier for so many years by assuming the best. He swung down and squatted on his heels, placing three fingertips lightly on the ground. He kept them there for a full two minutes.

"Feel anything?" Billy asked.

"The vibration is faint. It feels like a large group of riders, but I can't be sure they're headed in our direction."

Old Billy went a shade paler. "Out here, a big bunch of riders can only mean soldiers or Injuns. And since Injuns don't ride shod horses, the vibrations is always weaker."

"The way you say," Fargo agreed as he stepped up into leather and flicked the reins. "Keep a weather eye out."

The two men rode in silence for a spell, each alive with his own thoughts. The only sounds were the clinking of bit rings and the sleepy rhythm of hoof-clops.

"Fargo," Old Billy finally spoke up, "there's something cankering at me."

"You got a bone caught in your throat? Speak up."

"It's just—all these years I've knowed you and sided you in scrapes. You always been a man who believes in taking the bull by the horns."

Fargo nodded. "That's my credo."

"Sure, but look how it is now. Hell, I know that finding one man in this country is like trying to find a sliver in an elephant's ass. But you ain't said hardly nothin' about catching this woman-killin' bastard. Last night you swore up and down how that Doc Jacoby is the killer. Well, there we all was in the same canyon. Why in hell didn't you kill the scum-sucker—or at least find him and hog-tie him?"

Fargo's face suddenly looked tired. "I thought about it. But that would've meant barging in on camp after camp, calling attention to myself. Just shaving off my beard hardly makes me a new man. My map has been in newspapers all over the damn country thanks to these lying, nancy-boy ink-slingers. There's a good chance I could've been gut-shot without ever finding this filthy hyena."

Old Billy considered that and nodded. "Yeah, a place with that many people around ain't right for turning over rocks. But don't he have to be following us?"

"We plowed this ground before, chucklehead. Every swinging dick from London to New Orleans knows we're following the route of the Pony—and that route's been scattered, broadcast in newspapers, too."

"Hell, that's God's truth, ain't it? We're riding mostly at a trot and stopping now and again to study locations. That way he stays ahead of us and the trouble is waiting when we catch up to it."

"Trouble worse than a peeled rattler," Fargo agreed. Even as he said it, he glanced north again. The dust boiling on the horizon seemed darker and closer.

"I see it," Old Billy said without turning his head. "The trouble that don't wait for us is kind enough to ride and meet us. Best get your war face on, Fargo. I'd bet my bunions them's Utes coming to kill us."

The two men rated their horses at a good, hard gallop, searching for anyplace that might provide a natural bulwark. With the attacking Utes bearing down on them, they had to settle for scant cover—a small sand bench formed by the scouring wind.

Fargo swung down and broke out his glasses again. Now he could make out individual riders, their faces painted red and black. The large, heavily muscled brave out in front, wearing buffalo horns, was the battle chief.

"It's a raiding party," he reported. "I see plenty of trade rifles. They're not painted with war colors and they've got packhorses for booty. But the Utes know about white man's money, and they're dead set on getting ours."

Old Billy took the spyglasses from Fargo and took a look. He whistled sharply.

"Fargo, me and you is up against it bad! That's Spotted Pony and his bunch. I locked horns with them red sons once out near Robert's Creek. I was scouting for a freight caravan headed to Sacramento. They pinned us down for two days and killed four men. Lucky for us they run out of ammo and left."

"How many, you think?"

"Way the hell more than your reg'lar raiding party. Mebbe forty."

Fargo nodded. "That's my count, too. Thank God most tribes can't aim rifles like they can bows and arrows. Our only chance is to thin their ranks enough before they get close."

Old Billy nodded, taking Fargo's point. Most greenhorns back in the States believed that Indians commonly fought to the last man. But in truth they were highly spiritual and placed a great value on the lives of their own people. A battle leader who allowed too many braves to be killed faced grave censure in council.

While they spoke, the two experienced frontiersmen had pulled their saddles and laid out their weapons in the sand. Knowing their mounts would be early targets, they each threw an arm around their horse's neck and pulled them down to the ground. Both horses were trained to lie flat until pulled up again.

"Let's tote it up," Old Billy said. "Sixteen loads in your Henry, seven in my Spencer, six in your Colt plus that extra cylinder you got. I got six in my revolver and two in my Greener happens they get in close. That's . . . uh, that's . . . hell's bells, I never could cipher worth a damn."

"Forty-three shots before we have to reload," Fargo finished for him as the Utes pounded closer across the rugged Utah landscape. "But if we hold and squeeze, we should be able to turn them before we need reloads."

The bench offered scant protection, so both men began digging sand wallows with their hands. Spotted Pony, the battle chief, raised his rifle high and loosed a shrill, yipping war cry.

"I'd like to send that featherhead to the Land Beyond the Sun," Old Billy remarked. "Last time I waltzed with him he blew the tip of my left ear off. But we best leave him be— you know how the red Arabs get when you pop their leaders over."

"We got a little problem here, Billy," Fargo said. "It just occurred to me."

Old Billy jacked a round into the Spencer, then looked at Fargo. "What, you mean besides that whorehouse curtain you're wearing as a shirt?"

"That's one topic I'd avoid, I was you. No, I mean with our plan. I know how much you hanker to kill Indians, but in this case I think it just might cause us more trouble later. This bunch will wheel, all right, if we kill a few. But they'll keep coming back on a red vendetta. And we've got a long ride through empty spaces. They know they can eventually force us to use up our ammo—and then we're left like a bird's nest on the ground."

The first shot kicked up a geyser of dirt well out in front of them. Both men ignored it.

"Fargo, you got a point, and I'm caught upon it. That's ig-*zactly* the way Utes will play it. You got any big ideas?"

Fargo rested his right cheek on the stock of the Henry and sent a shot between the front feet of Spotted Pony's mount, slowing him down.

"The well's dry, partner. You're the specialist in Indian removal."

A sly grin came over Old Billy's face as he squeezed off a round, blowing a brave's rifle from his hands with the carbine's big slug. "I am, ain't I? Fargo, here's the way of it: Happens we kill enough Johns to drive them off, they'll be on us like ugly on a buzzard until they plant us. If we *don't* kill enough, they'll turn us into worm castles right here. Now you know what that means, don'tcha?"

Indian trade rifles were cracking loudly, most of the .31 caliber slugs whistling wide. But one thumped the ground near Fargo's head, throwing dirt into his eye. That brave was getting sassy and probing in close, so Fargo shot him in the foot and turned him.

"Big medicine?" he replied.

"*Big* medicine," Old Billy agreed, starting to inch backward toward his saddle. "Best way to drive Injuns off permanent like is to show them a sight they ain't never glommed before—most especial, a sight that shames their manhood. Keep them savages at bay, Fargo, until I get Richard out."

"Richard? Who the hell is he?"

"You're about to meet him. Just keep tossing lead."

By now Fargo was receiving as much as he tossed. A few of the better marksmen were sending rounds past his ears with a blowfly drone. He was grateful, however, that they had not yet gone into their highly favored circle attack with its ever-tightening noose.

The Henry bucked into his shoulder when he nicked a pony's pastern, spooking the mount into throwing his rider. When another crazy-brave Ute rushed him, Fargo drilled his right shoulder and spun him onto the ground.

"Let's get thrashing back there!" he shouted to Old Billy. "These ain't licorice drops they're throwing at us, and I can't keep winging them much longer. They push any closer, I'll have to kiss the mistress."

"Keep your pants on," Old Billy shot back, but when Fargo glanced over his shoulder he saw that the Indian fighter wasn't following his own advice—he had stripped buck naked and was now applying charcoal to his face—black, the color for celebrating the death of an enemy.

"You goddamn fool!" Fargo snapped. "Has your brain fried in this sun?"

He fired several more rounds, starting to ratchet up from nervous to desperate. When he glanced back Old Billy had risen to his feet—and Fargo was shocked sick and silly, his jaw dropping open. For a full ten seconds, despite the rounds parting his hair, he was speechless. He didn't know whether to laugh or puke—or both.

"How you like him?" Billy demanded as he strutted forward. "It's made of that India rubber—had her special-made in St. Louis."

Fargo had seen sights, during his wide travels, to make kings and queens marvel. He had seen streams in the Black Hills that actually ran uphill; grizzly bears so huge they could knock down a full-grown tree; prairie-dog towns in Texas that covered six hundred square miles; and buffalo herds so massive they took a full day to pass him. But *this* . . . it had no equal in his experience.

Old Billy's pale white body now sported a giant cod—huge in diameter, trailing almost to the ground, and quite realistic. It was trussed over his real sex with a flesh-colored band. To get the Utes' attention, Old Billy gyrated his hips and made the huge organ swing around like a tassel. As one, the braves stopped firing, stunned just like Fargo.

But Old Billy Williams wasn't content to shock them. He now pranced forward like a drunken madman, screaming Scripture.

"'Ye cannot drink the cup of the Lord and the cup of devils!'" he roared out.

Christ, they're going to shoot him, Fargo thought. *Hell, I might beat them to it.*

Old Billy gyrated his hips again, swinging the massive member as he hopped and pranced even closer. "'Ye cannot be partakers of the Lord's table and of the table of devils!'"

Fargo braced for the volley of shots, but it never came. Instead, Spotted Pony unleashed a shrill cry and the entire group whirled their ponies around, racing toward the north at a two twenty clip.

Old Billy swaggered back toward the sand wallows. "This ain't no dick," he declared proudly. "It's a Richard."

"*Sir* Richard," Fargo allowed, although he averted his eyes in disgust as he pushed to his feet.

76

"How's that for wit and wile?" Old Billy taunted him as he pulled Richard off and started dressing.

"It likely saved our lives," Fargo said, "but, William, you are one strange and sick son of a bitch."

Old Billy tossed back his head and howled like a wolf. "Hell yes I am! Always been, always be. But can any man say Billy Williams don't know his redskins?"

"Not around me," Fargo said. "Not that I ever doubted it."

Old Billy winked at Fargo. "I heard a couple sporting gals in Santa Fe talking you up, saying how you was 'well-endowed.' Don't looking at Richard make you feel a mite humble?"

Fargo grinned. "He does tend to give a man a puny feeling."

When he saddled his horse, Fargo sent a slanting glance toward Old Billy as he stuffed his giant rubber cod into a saddlebag.

"Old son," Fargo said quietly, "I don't mind if I die now for I have *truly* seen the elephant."

10

Deets Gramlich sat stunned in his saddle, still holding his telescope. He had acted in some wildly ribald skits in low theaters and barrelhouses from Manhattan to San Francisco. But what he had just witnessed was unsurpassed in his wide experience. He had been certain that Fargo and his partner were gone-up cases. Until . . . holy Jesus, until . . .

He suddenly burst into paroxysms of laughter that forced him to grip the horn. K.T. Christ! Those Indians had howled like dogs in the hot moons and fled quicker than scat. It wasn't just Fargo—this Old Billy Williams was savvy and cunning. Deets resolved yet again to exercise extreme caution. Otherwise he'd soon be playing checkers with the devil.

He sat his horse in the only concealed spot in sight, a narrow, shadowed declivity in the base of a mesa. Fargo and Williams were perhaps a mile north of his position, now bearing west toward Salt Lake City. This next attack, he mused, would have to be done with great precision and care. And this time he must toss a loop around Fargo, because Deets wanted nothing to do with the Great Salt Desert. His trail skills were top-notch, especially for a former thespian, but a trek across the Great Salt in search of suitable victims would be like searching for dictionaries in an Indian camp.

He turned the problem of Skye Fargo back and forth for a while. It disturbed his actor's vanity that Louise Tipton had doubted he was Fargo. By now Deets had come to believe that he *was* Fargo—believe it and like it. Before he had turned Fargo into a pariah, and it was safe to leave his Fargo disguise on, the power and pleasure had thrummed in his blood.

Beautiful women like Ginny Kreeger had sent him come-hither glances; capable frontiersmen jostled to buy him drinks. A man could get to like being Skye Fargo, all right.

Deets thought about that cretin Butch Landry and his two mangy sidekicks. So long as they kept doling out the gold cartwheels, he would do their bidding—Judge Moneybag ruled all his decisions. But their dream of seeing Fargo bouncing along in a tumbleweed wagon, on his way to a Mormon prison, would never pan out if Deets could grab the reins. If not, and Fargo did end up facing the gallows, at least there was the payoff.

Either way, Deets reminded himself as he sank steel into the ribs of his stallion, Skye Fargo was in one world of shit.

"I expected the grain to hold out longer," Fargo said as he and Old Billy broke camp on the fourth day after riding out from Fort Bridger. "Look at our mounts grazing saltbush."

"Them's tough horses," Old Billy reminded him. "Neither one of us coddles our mounts like them green-antlered fools who gives their horses names and feeds 'em sugar from their hands. Sugar—to a goddamn horse! I ain't had no sugar since Christ was a corporal."

"You damn piker, you won't lay out a few Bungtown coppers to buy a sack, that's all."

"Set it to music, why don'tcha? The hell you do with *your* money, bank it? Hell no! You piss it away on whiskey, whores, gambling, them fancy eating-houses where a Longhorn steak costs four bits. That time we run into each other in New Orleans, you had a hunnert dollars in your pocket. When I seen you two days later, you had to let a whore buy your breakfast."

Fargo grinned, shaking his head. "Old son, you're a caution to screech owls. You strap on a rubber pecker the size of a sequoia, prance around like a man from Bedlam, then lecture me on my wanton ways."

Old Billy joined the laughter. "Wa'n that the shits? Them damn Utes won't have the gumption to top their squaws for at least a moon."

"Anyhow," Fargo said, "that was yesterday. I have to plot down a couple more line stations today, and there's no way we'll make Salt Lake City before tomorrow. My Ovaro can get by on tree bark, but there's none to be had."

"Hell, my Appaloosa will eat tar-paper shingles," Old Billy boasted. "'Course, ain't none of them, neither. But, say! You ever heard tell of Kellar's Station?"

Fargo mulled it. "Well, once I knew a Junebug Kellar back in the Nebraska Territory. Big, pear-shaped fellow bald as a cue ball. He ran a ferry on the Niobrara."

"Yeah, that's Kellar. They taxed him outta Nebraska and he started out for the Sierra goldfields. But his back started givin' him jip, so he opened up a little station on the freight road, mebbe five, six miles from here. You seen his daughter?"

"He spoke of a little girl," Fargo replied. "I never saw her."

Old Billy grinned wickedly. "She ain't no little girl no more. Got a set of catheads on her what could derail a train."

Both men forked leather and gigged up their mounts.

"That's all real interesting," Fargo said, for he had not spent enough time with the tempting Caroline Reed back in Echo Canyon and now he regretted it. "But does Junebug sell grain?"

"His station is poor shakes, f'sure. Just a little clapboard shebang with a plank bar—he even sells liquor to Injuns so they won't lift his hair. Ain't no feed stable, but I recollect he sells oats and parched corn."

Fargo kept his head in constant motion, studying the bleak, parched terrain in the brassy morning sunlight.

"This could be a tricky piece of work," Fargo pointed out. "There's usually men lounging around these places, and Junebug knows both of us. And he's likely heard all the lies about my rape-and-killing spree."

Old Billy waved this aside. "Junebug won't credit the lies, not by a jugful. He knows how you saved all them orphans in the Dakota country."

"Maybe, but if he recognizes me even without my whiskers, he'll likely greet me by name. And even if he doesn't recognize me, he'll greet you by name. By now everybody knows that Old Billy Williams is siding me."

"You're a cheerful son of a bitch, Fargo," Billy said sarcastically. "We oughter get you a plug hat and a hearse."

"Just trying to wangle out of a bloodbath, old campaigner.

I haven't killed a soul since we took on this leg of the route, and I'd like to keep it that way."

Old Billy spat, again just missing the Ovaro's ear. "Why, you goddamn Quaker! Plenty of men require killing, and by God, I'm just the jasper to send 'em under."

"When you put it that way," Fargo replied, "I see the light. Hell, let's just chop wood and let the chips fall where they may."

"*Now* you're whistling! That first note you found called you death's second self."

That first note . . . now there, Fargo thought, was one pig's afterbirth who definitely required killing. But could he be stopped before it was too late? Fargo had confidence in his ability to square off against any man. But how could he cut sign on a man who lived in the shadows—or draw down on a man who was only *odjib*, a thing of smoke?

Once a man mates with despair, he's worthless. An old mountain man had told Fargo that many years ago, and the Trailsman had rallied himself many times with those words. But this evil preying on him now was different. A soulless coward was turning Fargo against himself, turning a rough-hewn but decent frontiersman into a despicable pariah in the eyes of the world.

"Keep up the strut," he muttered. "Straight ahead."

"What's that?" Old Billy demanded. "Speak out like a man or go braid your pigtails."

"I said, I think I'll find out where you hide your money and steal it."

Even Old Billy's purple birthmark turned pale. In a flash he drew his fancy Brasher of London six-gun.

"Long Shanks, don't you *even* joke about my money. You ever touch it, I'll kill you deader than last Christmas."

Five seconds of silence except for the *ching*ing bit rings. Then both men broke into raucous laughter.

"Kellar's Station dead ahead," Old Billy said a minute later. "Knock that riding thong off your hammer, Quaker, and let's commence to killing."

Across the dust-hazed sage, shimmering like a heat mirage in the metallic sun, Fargo spotted a typical frontier shebang leaning under the weight of shoddy construction and too much wind. Jagged pieces of flock board had been cobbled together to make walls, and a stovepipe chimney rose through a roof of flattened vegetable cans. Fargo counted four horses at the mesquite tie-rail out front.

Old Billy spat a brown streamer, this one so close to the Ovaro's right ear that the stallion whinnied in warning.

"You'll regret that reckless spitting," Fargo assured him. "That pinto is mighty touchy about his ears."

"The hell! He's fine horseflesh, but the *rider* is the master. Consarn you, Fargo, flush out your headpiece. Ain't no mother-ruttin' horse lays down the law to Old Billy Williams."

Fargo bit his lip to keep a straight face. "All right, then. I've brought it up twice and I won't harp on it anymore."

"Huh. You just watch me—*you* might have this animal lipping salt from your hand, but by God he'll dance when I pipe."

"Four horses tied off ahead," Fargo remarked. "Let's reconnoiter soon as we go inside just in case they're hungry for a frolic. I like to know what kind of artillery might open up on me."

Old Billy grinned. "Say! Why don't we just go in a-smokin' like we done in that cantina in El Paso? Brother, them Mexican slavers didn't know whether to piss or go blind. Lead was flying ever which-way before you even slapped the batwings."

Fargo laughed at the memory. "Yeah, and you singing '*La Paloma*' in Spanish. But this is different—we might kill Junebug or his girl. And from what you said about her tits—"

Fargo stopped in midsentence, watching four heavily armed men who had just emerged into the glaring sun. They stood only twenty yards away, rifles and scatterguns trained on the new arrivals.

"Shit-oh-dear," Old Billy muttered. "We was so busy flap-jawin' I forgot to break out Patsy."

"This won't be a wit-and-wile situation," Fargo muttered back. "Look for the main chance, Old Billy, then spark your powder."

The two men reined in, dust swirling around them in the hot wind.

"Don't stop there," said a toothless chawbacon dressed in butternut homespun. "Climb off them hosses and lead 'em in."

Both men ignored the order. Old Billy hunched forward in the saddle, trying to see better in the blowing dust. "Horten? Zachary Horten, is that you?"

"A-huh," Horten replied in his High South twang, keeping his close-set eyes narrowed on Fargo. "You're free to ride on, Old Billy. Ain't nobody said a word agin you. It's Skye Fargo here what faces a reckonin'."

"Fargo! Hell, I got shed of him miles back. This here is Frank Scully."

Horten shook his head. "Best be careful, Billy, or we *will* have a score to settle with you for sidin' with a rapist and woman-killer."

The man beside Horten, a hatchet-faced *mestizo* in a raw-wool serape, spoke up. "Word came from Echo Canyon, Fargo, that you shaved your beard and got new clothes."

"Yeah, shit-for-brains," spoke up a third man, gawking at the shirt. "You'd a been less conspicuous in your buckskins than in that nigger-woman blouse."

"Man ain't got no taste," Old Billy muttered to Fargo.

"Light down," Horten ordered again, wagging the barrel of his New Haven Arms rifle. "First, Fargo, we're gonna learn you that wimmin is respected in the Utah Territory. After that, you'll dance on air. Then me and the boys here will draw cards to see who gets that fine horse of yours."

"That's all I was waiting to hear," Fargo said quietly.

"How's that?"

"I wanted it to be legal," Fargo explained, "so I waited until you threatened my life."

Quicker than eyesight, Fargo filled his fist with blue steel. The Colt bucked in his hand and a neat hole opened in the center of Horten's forehead. Blood blossomed out, splashing into the parched earth with a sound like a horse pissing. Fargo's reflexive speed, and the sudden fact of death in their midst, froze the other three men like statues of salt.

By the time the other three were able to blink again, Old

Billy had his Greener unsheathed and at the ready. "Drop 'em, boys," he ordered in his gravelly voice. "If the Cheyenne Dog Soldiers couldn't spill my guts, you three bald-headed baboons sure as hell won't, neither."

Facing this double threat, all three complied instantly.

Old Billy laughed so hard he was forced to slap his thigh. "Fargo, these needle-dick bug-humpers won't never learn territorial law. Back in the States they got that 'duty to retreat' law if a man's life is threatened. Out here, a threat ain't no different than the attempt. This fool ain't the first to turn his tongue into a shovel and bury hisself with it."

"Hop your horses and clear out," Fargo told them. "We'll take your weapons inside, and you can collect them tomorrow. If you show up here while I'm still around, I'll kill you for cause."

"Before you ride out," added a voice from the doorway of the station, "haul that body down the road a piece so I don't have to sniff the stink. Let the buzzards bury the blowhard son of a bitch."

Fargo swung down, looking at a pear-shaped, bald-headed man in a filthy apron. "Junebug Kellar. Glad to see the citizen's committee here didn't douse your light."

"They threatened to if I shouted a warning. Skye goldang Fargo . . . I haven't seen you since the hogs ate the twins. Chappie, you been getting into a heap of trouble lately."

"Somebody else is doing all the work, Junebug. I just reap the benefits."

Junebug looked askance at Fargo's haberdashery. "Christ, that's the kind of shirt you see in nightmares. And if them pants was any tighter your voice would change."

"I *like* them, Pa," said a lilting female voice from behind Junebug.

Fargo watched a stunning young redhead, in a worn print dress so thin it fit like a second skin, ease around her father and into the doorway. Either she didn't like undergarments or she couldn't get any out here because Fargo could see all of her ample charms—everything from her supple calves to the two spots where her nipples dinted the fabric of her dress.

"Skye," Junebug said, "this is my girl, Jasmine—the one you know as little Jasmine. She's a mite bigger now."

"I see that," Fargo said, barely able to lift his eyes from her swelling bosom.

With Billy and his Greener supervising, the three would-be hangmen were hauling the body of Zachary Horten well down the trail.

"Mr. Fargo," Jasmine chirped, giving him a teasing look from lidded eyes, "I thought you had a beard."

"I did," he said ruefully, rubbing his stubbled chin. "That's before I became a desperado."

"You look fine without one," she assured him.

"You best take a care, Skye," Junebug spoke up. "The whole damn territory is boiling over. This is the second rope posse that's been in here to ask about you."

"How 'bout Mormon soldiers?"

"Ain't seen hide nor hair of any in weeks. They been busy with Ute uprisings around Camp Floyd."

"It does beat all," Jasmine chimed in, "that men who beat the tar out of their women every day get so high and mighty all of a sudden. Maybe they got some other reason for wanting to kill Mr. Fargo—one their women could explain."

Her eyes traveled his length—quite a journey. "Pa's right about them clothes. But the man inside them is mighty easy to look at. Now I seen him, Pa, I know you're right. This is no fella who'd ever need to . . . force a woman."

"You're right on that score, sugar britches," called out Old Billy as he watched the trio of vigilantes ride off. "Women flock to him like flies to honey. But he has to get rough with barnyard animals."

Junebug chortled and Fargo grinned at the vulgar lout. Jasmine was too busy playing kissy-face with Fargo to even notice Old Billy. At the moment Fargo regretted that—in these molded-on pants his arousal was obvious. Casually, he brought his hat down over his crotch.

Old Billy hadn't missed the concealment. "She might be impressed, Fargo, but Sir Richard ain't."

"Who's Sir Richard?" asked a confused Jasmine.

"Oh, this gent I know," Old Billy replied, barely keeping a straight face. "You could call him a mite cocky."

"Sorry if we chased away your business," Fargo said as he followed the owner and his daughter into the dark, hot, smoky interior. Old dry-goods boxes served as chairs, but somewhere Junebug had scrounged up an old billiard table. It sported bullet holes and patched felt.

Junebug snorted. "Business? All that bunch ever done was swill whiskey on account and never pay me. Only reason they come is to ogle Jasmine."

"And pinch me," she added. "But I won't . . . get friendly with any man who ain't got nice teeth. Strong and white like yours, Mr. Fargo."

Junebug waved his daughter silent. "Honey, I told you before, you're of age and I don't begrudge your little flirtations. But wait till your daddy ain't around. And you can call him Skye—me and him go way the hell back."

He turned to Fargo. "You're in sore need of a bath. And I got some duds that might fit you—nothing too fancy-fine, but hell, least you won't look like a circus juggler."

"'Preciate it. How's your tarantula juice?"

"Never mind that, you damn criminal," Old Billy cut in. "I'll test the who-shot-john while you get that bath. Happens you hear gunfire up here, fill your hand and fill it quick."

11

"C'mon," Jasmine told him, taking Fargo's hand, "I'll show you where everything is."

Fargo could see where everything was, all right, and he liked the placement just fine. As she tugged him toward a lean-to off the back of the station, he watched her tight buttocks undulate against the thin dress like two melons shifting in a sack.

Just outside the lean-to was a flat-iron stove. A bucket next to it was stuffed with corncobs soaking in coal oil. She banged open the door of the stove and threw some cobs in.

Fargo peeked down the front of her dress as she bent down and got an eye-filling peek at her creamy, plum-tipped tits.

"Like 'em?" she asked as she struck a phosphor on the stove and flipped it onto the fuel.

"You know I do. What red-blooded man wouldn't?"

She tossed back her head and laughed. "Pa's right. All men want the same thing."

Fargo began hauling water from a nearby cistern. "What's wrong with that? Don't women want the same thing, too?"

"Of course we do. But men just go right at it like bulls to a red rag. Women have a different style."

"Oh?" Fargo said with mock innocence as he poured a pail of water into the larger heating pan on the stove. "I hadn't noticed."

She laughed again and slugged him on the arm. "No need to play the preacher, Mr. Fargo—I mean, Skye. Pa tells me you been with more women than a midwife."

"The only one that counts," he assured her, "is the one you're with now."

87

"And tomorrow she's a memory, right?"

"A memory for life," he assured her, although in fact only the best of the best became that.

Soon the water was hot and Fargo hauled it to the washtub in the lean-to, pouring it in.

"There's lye soap on that shelf beside you," she said, "and a scrap of towel. I'm gonna go dig up them duds pa mentioned."

He unbuckled his gun belt and dropped it beside the tub. As he stripped out of the odious clothing and eased into the water, Fargo wasn't sure there was any fire behind Jasmine's smoke. He had indeed been with many women, and it wasn't always the ones who acted most forward who were quick to drop their linen. Besides, the idea of tupping a gal with her father only a few feet away didn't appeal to him—and that barren landscape outside hardly offered a leafy bower as love nest.

He could hear Old Billy's voice rising and getting more belligerent—the damn piker was getting drunk on free liquor. Fargo had to lather his sweaty, oily hair twice before it felt clean. He dunked his head to rinse it, and when he sat up cold steel kissed his left temple.

"Shit," he said calmly, waiting for the bright-orange starburst inside his skull that signaled the end of the trail.

"Bang," Jasmine said, tittering. "You're dead."

"Why, you little vixen!"

Fargo grabbed the weapon from her and set it aside, then pulled her into the tub dress and all. He began smacking her soundly on that Georgia-peach ass, hard, resounding slaps that made her cry out in protest and wiggle like a puppy.

"Whale her a few for me, Skye!" Junebug shouted. "I've spared the rod too long with that sassy brat!"

Jasmine suddenly stopped squirming as her hand found Fargo's shaft. "*Here's* a rod we don't need to spare. Land o'Goshen, Skye, why's it so big and hard?"

"Same reason that spanking was so long—I liked what I was feeling."

"You prob'ly like these, too, huh?"

Sloshing water over the brim of the tub, she shimmied until her dress was down to her hips. Fargo was duly impressed with the two puffy loaves with cocoa rings circling the protuberant nipples.

"I can't decide if I really like them until I sample them," he assured her, bending his sopping head down to take one of the nipples into his mouth. He sucked and kissed it, throwing in a few nibbles for good measure. Undaunted by the crowd in the tub, she sighed and wiggled her butt.

"Yeah, I like 'em," he finally reported.

She still had his turgid manhood gripped in her hand. When she tipped it back, Fargo's length made it easily clear the water.

"Think I'll return the favor," she told him breathlessly, her hair fanning out in the water as she lowered her heart-shaped lips onto him and began bobbing for apples. The part she couldn't get into her mouth she gripped with a thumb and forefinger, forming a tight cinch and pumping her hand up and down.

Fargo squirmed at the hot, tight, liquid pleasure pouring over his man gland. He interlaced his fingers in her thick hair and guided her as she got up a head of steam, fire on fire to the fuel inside him. The explosion began as a hot glow in his groin, a glow that turned into a tickling prickle that pulsed between his balls and his shaft.

She felt him growing iron hard in her mouth and moaned with excitement. Her head was bobbing as quick as a steam piston, her hand moving with a blur of speed. The pleasure in his staff finally reached its peak and Fargo exploded with a mighty gasp, hips bucking a dozen times before he made his conclusive thrust. Then he collapsed into the water like a rag puppet.

"My stars and garters!" she exclaimed through the delirium of his pleasure. "You ain't gone soft one bit! 'Pears I'll have to straddle you and tame that hungry beast."

Fargo was helping her mount him when Old Billy's sly voice roared out, "Fargo, you're burning daylight! You've soaped your ears enough. Them three shit-kickers we sent packing will come back with a mob. The longer we tarry here, the more danger we put Junebug and Jasmine in. Time to light a shuck out of here."

"Tell that old stain face to piss up a rope," Jasmine pleaded.

"He's right," Fargo said reluctantly. "He's always right at the wrong times."

"Ain't no fair," she pouted. "We didn't even get to screw. I'll have a bellyache all night."

Fargo lifted her out of the tub, her wet dress clinging like a can label, and climbed out behind her. "I don't like it either, cupcake. You are one fine specimen of woman."

This cheered her up a bit. Fargo dried off with a rough, thin towel, then looked at the clothes she handed him: a pair of worn but clean kersey trousers and a cotton pullover shirt.

"Nothing fancy," she said, "but lots better than them ridiculous rags you got on."

"The way you say," Fargo replied gratefully, pulling them on. "Fit better, too."

"Kind of a shame," she teased him, glancing at the looser-fitting trousers. "Least them others didn't leave much to a gal's imagination."

"Fargo, you skunk-bit coyote!" Old Billy's gravelly voice roared. "This ain't no foofaraw house! If you ain't horsed in one minute, I'll come back there and shoot you to doll stuffings!"

The vast Mormon region formerly known as Deseret had become the Utah Territory in 1850. The Mormons had been forced to endure some gentiles as government officers, but the Saints still controlled the city and made sure there were few attractions to draw the lower elements. Destitute travelers, especially women and children, were generously assisted, but saloons were almost nonexistent, and fornication was strictly forbidden by law so that soiled doves were never spotted on the wide streets.

There were, however, clean camps provided for outlanders on the edge of the sprawling city. Riding hard from Echo Canyon, swinging well south to avoid Skye Fargo and his dangerous friend, Butch Landry's gang reached one of these camps on the evening of the day Fargo had visited Kellar's Station.

"Butch," Orrin Trapp carped, kicking at the fire, "I ain't never seen the like of these Mormons! The men all got them beards that look like half a doughnut, and the women—Christ! Buncha sour-pussed old biddies that look like their assholes are screwed on too tight. Hell, I kept gettin' 'em mixed up with the oxen they got all over this town."

"Never mind that," Butch snapped. "Didja find a bottle?"

"Are you shittin'? Every Jack shall have his Jill before you find any strong water in this town. I found one saloon, but all they had was beer and sarsaparilla."

"See how it is?" Butch stewed. "When it comes to women, these Mormon men run a whole string just for theirselves. But can a bachelor passing through town find a saloon with gals topside? Hypocritical sons of bitches."

He spat into the fire and heaved a long sigh. "Well, good chance Fargo will be in this area by tomorrow. If Deets does his job good—and he has so far—we won't need to be here all that long. Just long enough to see Fargo clamped into chains and tossed into prison. Trials ain't delayed around here, boys, and the lawyers are all Mormons. When we know the hanging date, we'll come back for that, too. Maybe even piss on Fargo's grave."

"Say," Orrin piped up, "when Fargo goes to prison, we need to visit him—just so he'll know who done him in before he stretches hemp."

Landry laughed long and hard. "Orrin, you struck a lode there! Ain't a damn thing he can do about it by then. But wait . . . that might not be a smart play seeing as how we're all wanted, too."

"We'll send in a note after we're long gone," Orrin suggested. "We won't spell it out plain—just something to let him know it was us that cooked his goose to a cinder."

The men quieted down as a Mormon constable rode past on a big sorrel, casting a suspicious glance in their direction. The camps were free, firewood provided, but any violation of the rules and they'd get the boot.

"Brigham Young's lick-finger," Orrin muttered.

"Bluenoses all," Butch agreed. "But we dursn't get pinched—these law-and-order bastards run files on every wanted man in the territory. I prefer a bullet to the brain over going back to prison."

Harlan Perry, squatting by the fire and gnawing on a cold biscuit, spoke up. "How's Deets gonna nab a young girl in a place like this? Hell, everybody stares at any outsider and I didn't see no gals walking the streets except prune-faced biddies."

"He won't do it here in the city," Butch replied. "North of here, still in Salt Lake Valley near the lake, there's this settlement called Mormon Station. It's for tending crops in the valley. Deets says it ain't much more than a double handful of cabins strung along an irrigation canal."

"But that lake is salt water," Orrin said.

"Yeah, but they got a snowmelt reservoir up there. That's how's come they got all they rye and wheat fields. Anyhow, Deets has already been through there and met a little gal named Rebecca who don't exactly live by the Book of Mormon, if you take my drift. He figures he can lure her out—him disguised as Fargo, of course—and cut up rough—rough enough that Mormon law will throw a net around the real Fargo."

"But if he kills her," Orrin put in, "how will anybody know Fargo done it?"

"He don't need to kill her. Rape is a hanging offense around here. But he's gonna cut her up so bad that she'll have to talk out."

"Hell, that's all right, I s'pose," Harlan said. "I mean, Butch, it was your brother Fargo killed, and he put all of us in prison to boot, so t'hell with him. But I sure will be glad to get shed of all this skulkin' around and get back to the States—we got all that gold and we ain't hardly had no chance to spend it."

"You and me have hitched our thoughts to the same post," Butch said. "Money is like manure—it works best when you spread it around. And just as soon as Fargo has started his one or two years of penitence, we'll point our bridles due east. Saint Louis, maybe, or hell, maybe even go west to San Francisco. That way the trip will be shorter when Fargo gets jerked to Jesus."

"What about Deets?" Orrin said quietly.

Butch searched for his foxlike features in the yellow-orange firelight. "How's that?"

"Deets. What happens with him at the end of the trail?"

"Why, we square up with him. What else?"

"That's cussed stupidity," Orrin said bluntly. "That theater fop is shiftier than a creased buck. The moment he gets his last yeller boy from us, he could turn around and collect the reward on us."

"How?" Harlan demanded. "Lookit all the crimes he done for us."

"Besides," Butch said, "how can he work a double-cross on us when he's wanted for murder himself? Killed a gal beloved all over San Francisco—all on account she wouldn't let him court and spark her. So it's a standoff between us and him."

"Maybe so," Orrin conceded, "but I say we just kill the son of a bitch. He knows too much. Besides, we not only save the final payment, we're likely to find most of the gold we paid him so far. I don't like that high-hatting bastard. Thinks his shit don't stink just because he can rattle off Shakespeare. Hell, any gal-boy can read a book and get it off by heart."

"Deets ain't no gal-boy," Butch said with conviction. "He's all grit and a yard wide. Still, I think Orrin is on to a scent. When you send a man as famous as Skye Fargo to the gallows, it ain't smart to have a man like Deets running around knowing about it. What if he makes a deathbed confession?"

"Now you're talking sense," Orrin approved. "Best way to cure a boil is to lance it."

Butch slowly nodded, his face brooding in the flickering firelight. "But let's take care of Fargo first—he's the biggest frog in the puddle."

12

Fargo and Old Billy managed to locate and record one more future line station before grainy twilight descended on them, bringing a blessed chill with it. Because of the threat of Mormon soldier patrols, triggered by the recent Ute uprisings, they opted for a cold camp in a slight hollow just off the federal freight road about ten miles east of Salt Lake City.

"We got one helluva piece of work ahead of us," Old Billy remarked as the two men shared an airtight of peaches they had purchased from Junebug Kellar. "You can say what you want to about the queer ways of Mormons; they ain't no fools, not by a jugful."

"I never said they were," Fargo replied, slurping some juice from the can. "Matter of fact, I like Mormons all right. They've hired me several times and always paid good money."

"Well, ain't that just sweet lavender?" Billy spat out sarcastically. "Fargo likes the Mormons. That ain't the point, bonehead. Happens you done work for them, we're in even deeper shit than I thought—that means they recognize your face. I done looked at that route map of yours, and damn my eyes if we ain't riding damn near into the city itself."

"Is that too rich for your belly, Indian fighter? You're the one harping how we have to get the job done so you can draw your wages. You got some plan for us to just fly over the city?"

Old Billy cursed. "Fargo, you are the world-beatingest man I ever wanted to shoot. You know what I mean. Ain't nobody left on God's green earth what don't know who's mapping out these line stations. We'll be marked for carrion the minute we ride in."

Fargo wiped his hands on his new trousers and settled back against his saddle. "All right, so what's your big idea?"

"Simple—we *don't* ride in. The line station can be before or after the city itself. So we either site it to the east or west. Either way, we can swing south of the settlement and never set a hoof in it."

"We could," Fargo agreed. "But what happened to the blustering bravo who was roweling me to lock horns with this Fargo imposter?"

"Huh?"

"You yourself said it, Billy. Salt Lake City is really his last chance to get me framed for good. After that is just god-awful desert and empty Sierra until Sacramento. I'd say he's going to do his level best in Salt Lake, wouldn't you?"

Fargo could see Old Billy in the buttery moonlight, pulling on his chin and thinking. "I can't gainsay it. But what if he does attack a Mormon woman? Mister, happens he does, I'd ruther be caught in a buffalo stampede than in Salt Lake City."

"I already told you how the whole city foolishly sees me as a sort of savior—that time when a swarm of grasshoppers had descended on the crops in the valley."

Old Billy snorted. "That claptrap about how, just as you come over the ridge, all the seagulls rose up from the lake and et all the grasshoppers? Don't make me pop a rib laughing. Tell me, Fargo, did you ride around the lake or walk across it?"

"I said it was foolishness, didn't I? It was just coincidental timing, but all religions believe in miracles, and the Saints decided I was a miracle worker."

"Uh-huh, just like the miracle you worked in that wash-tub earlier, Saint Fargo. All right, so these blame fool Mormons think you're a first cousin to Jesus. Don't forget, they been hearing all kinds of swamp gas lately about how Skye Fargo has turned into a rapist and murderer. Then you sashay into town and—likely—a Mormon gal gets attacked. You really think that plague-of-locusts twaddle will keep you— maybe *us*—out of the noose?"

"No," Fargo admitted readily. "That's why I have another plan, too. It's mainly the Ovaro that gets us scrutinized right off. And by now they know about your Appaloosa. There's a big livery on the outskirts of the city run by an old codger named Mica Jones—if he's still above the earth. We can trust him. We'll ride in after dark and leave our horses there, rent two from him."

"New horses would help," Old Billy agreed. "And you got them duds that don't make you look like a Bowery pimp, and with your whiskers gone and all—still, it could be a wild and bloody business."

"Would you have it any other way?"

Old Billy howled like a wolf. "*Hell* no! I've killed more red savages, and pronged more plump squaws, than any swinging dick in the West! I can kill a grizz with a butter knife, bring down a bull buffalo with my bolos, and piss across the Missouri! Fargo, if them wivin' Mormons do kill you, I'll drink your goddamn blood and make an ammo pouch outta your scrote."

"*That's* the Old Billy I know and love," Fargo said fondly. "But nix on the ammo pouch."

"It was an ammo pouch today," Old Billy said slyly. "All I could hear back in that lean-to was heavy breathin' and water sloshin'. How was she, boy?"

"That's a mite hard to say," Fargo admitted. "As far as we got, she was fine."

"Ah-*hah*! So there's one filly the stallion couldn't mount."

"How could I with you threatening to shoot me if I didn't get a wiggle on?"

Even in the moonlit darkness, Fargo saw the astounded look on Old Billy's homely face. "Why, God's garters, I gave you fifteen minutes! How much time do you need in the rut? Christ, I've topped three Mandan squaws in the time it takes to eat a biscuit."

"Billy, it takes most women a little longer to get their shiver than it does men. I like to leave 'em eager in case I see them again."

This remark landed on Old Billy like a bomb. He pushed to his feet and stood over Fargo with arms akimbo. "Fargo, what is wrong with you and what doctor told you so? Why, the woman ain't nothing to the matter. You think a male dog holds off to please the bitch? This is what comes of petticoat guv'ment."

Fargo waved him back down, laughing. "Never mind, you cantankerous fool. I just want to warn you again—I see you're spitting closer and closer to the Ovaro's ear, taunting him. Ease off or you'll rue the day."

"Listen to this jay! 'Bout what I'd expect from a man what thinks a woman deserves a 'shiver' when he tops her. You mollycoddle that damn animal, Fargo, that's the long and short of it. By God, he'll be broke to saddle *and* master when I'm through with him."

Fargo grinned wickedly in the darkness. "All right," he said mildly. "You might be right, at that."

They had purchased a sack of oats at Kellar's Station. Fargo fed and watered both horses from his hat while Old Billy softened ground for their bedrolls. But as Fargo worked he gazed in the direction of Salt Lake City, wondering: Was the man who signed himself Death's Second Self already at work?

Later, the words of the killer's second note chased Fargo down a long tunnel into sleep:

The curtain's coming down, Fargo.

The fifth day of Fargo's relentless struggle against an unseen foe dawned somber and hot, with rain clouds piling up like boulders on the horizon. With time to spare before they rode into Salt Lake City after sunset, Fargo put his sharp eye and prodigious tracking skills to work.

When they were about five miles northeast of the city, Fargo tugged rein and guided Billy's Appaloosa toward the south.

"How's come we're leaving the freight road?" Old Billy demanded. "I thought you was figuring to cut sign on this twin of yours?"

"I am. But do you really think he'll just waltz into Salt Lake City on the main trail? He's not likely disguised as me all the time, especially now, but he's riding a stallion that fits the Ovaro's description."

"That ciphers. You always was a better hand than me at tracking, Fargo."

Fargo glanced at the gray, bleak morning sky. Those ragged black clouds on the horizon were now rapidly blowing off without dumping rain. But the stiff wind that propelled them was also scouring the barren plain that rimmed Salt Lake Valley, obscuring any prints.

For nearly two hours the men walked their horses at a right angle to the freight road, Fargo leaning low out of the saddle and minutely studying the ground. Now and then he swung down and hunkered on his heels, searching closer.

"Somebody walked a horse in from the south," he said at one point, "but the hooves are unshod."

"Mountain Utes from the Wasatch Range," Old Billy said matter-of-factly. "I seen 'em work this grift before. They make attacks on the outposts and lure the soldiers up into the mountains in pursuit. But they keep a band down here to hit the freight wagons."

Fargo nodded and climbed up onto the hurricane deck. "The city is safe, though. Even without the Mormon Battalion there's enough firepower here to start a war with Europe."

"Uh-huh. 'Sides, your average Red John won't attack even a small town. The buildings scare the shit outta them. But that firepower might be turned on *us*, Trailsman, in a puffin' hurry."

But Fargo ignored him, swinging down again and squatting over a gravel seam. Old Billy joined him.

"The hell, Fargo! What you glommin' so close? All I see is dirt and gravel."

Fargo outlined a dim print with his finger. "It's fresh—the edges haven't crumbled. But the damn wind is filling it in."

"Is it our killer?"

Finally Fargo nodded. "I'd lay good odds. This is the rear offside shoe, and it's loose."

Eyes closed to slits, Fargo glanced ahead into the swirling dust and gravel. "No sense trying to follow him. This print only lasted because of the gravel, and there's nothing but sand ahead. The wind will wipe 'em out."

"He must be a blame fool," Old Billy pointed out. "Riding that marked horse straight into the city. Or do you figure he went in at night?"

"The print was likely made last night, but I don't think he headed into the city. The course he's riding would likely take him south of the city and up to Mormon Station near the lake."

Old Billy rubbed his chin. "Where it'll be easier to rape and kill."

"Seems to me it won't be easy, and he won't kill. He could shoot from ambush, sure, but that's not what he's after. He wants to leave a raped and badly hurt woman to testify that Skye Fargo attacked her."

Fargo forked leather. "Much as I hate to let it happen, we've got no choice. If we go charging in there now, we'll just get shot or jugged."

They gigged their mounts in the direction the mystery outlaw had taken.

"If we ain't gonna stick our noses into the pie," Old Billy said, "why're we dogging him?"

"We have to do something," Fargo replied. "We can sneak up through the salt dunes and get a good look at the valley and Mormon Station. He'll likely wait until tonight to make his move. If I spot the son of a bitch, I'm gonna kill him and drag his body into the middle of the city. Let them get a good gander at 'death's second self.'"

The sun returned with a vengeance as the last, swift-moving storm clouds blew to the east. The sky had cleared to a deep, gas-flame blue, and purple-hazed mountains marched along distant horizons.

The two riders stayed far enough back from the city to be obscured in the brilliant glare reflecting off quartz and mica in the sand. The conical dunes provided excellent cover as they ascended to the lip of the valley.

They finally cleared a long, sloping ridge and even jaded Old Billy gawped in amazement at sight of the fertile valley. It was shaped like a giant amphitheater and ringed completely by mountains. Thanks to irrigation it was brilliant with green grass and large fields of cucumbers, melons, and squash, separated by grape-stake fences. Fargo spotted cattle, hogs, chickens, turkeys, all of excellent quality. Broadleaved cottonwoods and tall poplars, while not profuse, were a welcome sight for destitute travelers approaching from the arid and featureless Salt Desert west of the city.

"You can't say the Saints ain't hard workers," Old Billy begrudged. "Damn! I'd give a party for one a them melons."

"Yeah, Mormons have no need of clocks," Fargo agreed. "The workday goes on from can to can't. Only way to whip a desert."

Just then Fargo felt a familiar "goose tickle" on the back of his neck—a feeling he had learned to respect.

"Pull back a little," he told Old Billy. "You're skylined."

"Kiss my lily-white hinder, rapist," Old Billy replied, though he did cluck to the Ovaro, backing up.

Fargo reached across to his own saddle and pulled the field glasses out. Careful not to let them reflect, he began studying the entire valley.

"Nothing's happened yet," he decided. "Or else, it hasn't been discovered yet. Nothing but hard work going on below."

"Then where's he laid up?" Old Billy demanded.

"He could be holed up anywhere—laying down in a field, up one of those cottonwoods, maybe even in a root cellar. But where the hell's his horse?"

Old Billy shook his head. "That's a sticker, all right. Fargo. I ain't one for spirit knockin's and such, but this old hoss commences to wonder if we're up agin a damn ghost."

Fargo, still feeling a tickle on his nape, reined the Appaloosa around to study the long line of dunes behind them. Just for a heartbeat reflected light winked from one of them.

"The hell you eyeballing?" Old Billy demanded.

Fargo opened his mouth to reply when a rifle cracked, sending loud echoes out over the valley.

13

"Here's the fandango!" Fargo shouted almost joyously, recognizing the distinctive sound of a Henry repeater and guessing his deadly imposter had finally confronted him.

Even as he spoke he jerked his feet from the stirrups and tossed the reins to Old Billy. He reached over and snatched his own Henry from its boot and jacked a round into the chamber.

"Get those horses to the other side of the dune," he ordered Billy. "Then bring your Greener."

A fractional second after he finished speaking, the Henry erupted with another concussive, ear-splitting crack. "Jesus!" Fargo muttered when the bullet nicked the bow of the Appaloosa's saddle, then sent up a geyser of salt dust when it punched into the ground.

Old Billy wheeled the Ovaro around and slapped his glossy rump, leading both mounts to safety. All of this took only a few seconds, and there was still a black feather of telltale powder smoke marking the shooter's position. Fargo, realizing by now the hidden man had no plans to kill him, guessed that his real target was Old Billy—a dangerous sidekick and one well worth removing.

Fargo took up a kneeling-offhand position, dropped the Henry's front sight on the edge of that dune, and peppered it with eight quick shots. Again the shooter's Henry spoke its piece, but the bullets hit the dirt wide of Fargo. He's waiting for Billy, Fargo realized.

The moment Old Billy appeared, Fargo grabbed the scattergun and handed his partner the Henry. "Cover fire, old son," he ordered Billy. "I'm charging the son of a bitch. Right now we just want to make him rabbit—those settlers in the valley are sounding their horn, and they'll be on us quicker than a finger snap. And *don't* give him a target—it's you he's trying to plug."

With Old Billy spraying the dune from a prone position, Fargo ran forward in a low crouch, thumb-cocking both hammers. He steadied the gun in his hip socket and twitched one trigger. The shotgun kicked hard and the spray of 12-gauge buckshot blew a melon-sized chunk out of the dune. He blasted it again and tossed the Greener aside, shucking out his Colt and hoping for a showdown.

But when he rounded the mutilated dune, no one was in sight. Nor did he hear a horse retreating.

"Time to dust our hocks!" Old Billy shouted behind him. "We got five Mormons with rifles riding this way and they ain't looking to convert us!"

Fargo cursed. This was an excellent opportunity to cut sign on the elusive criminal. But falling into Mormon hands right now, especially appearing as if he had disguised himself, was no sane option. He quickly rejoined Old Billy.

"Most of these Mormon horses are just plow nags," he said as he swung up into leather on Billy's Appaloosa. "We'll head across the desert toward the mountains. They don't know what was going on up here, so I don't figure they'll chase us that long. If they do, a few snapshots should reverse their dust."

Unless, Fargo reminded himself, somebody got word to the military barracks near City Creek. If that happened, they were in for a merry chase.

Fargo had called it right. The Mormon farmers, realizing they were up against two fast horses, gave up the chase before it even began. Fargo and Old Billy, riding slow in the furnace heat of Salt Desert, hooked wide to the west of the city looking for a suitable place to hole up until nightfall.

"You think them dirt-scratchers mighta recognized your stallion?" Old Billy asked, trying to spit but failing.

"I think we had too much of a lead," Fargo replied. "But I fear they'll soon know Skye Fargo is around—just as soon as that dry-gulching bastard attacks again disguised as me."

"Ain't it just the drizzlin' shits? You know the poison-mean snake is gonna strike again, but you can't show your pan to stop it. It's a jo-fired mess."

"I'm not so sure I can't show my pan," Fargo said. "If I'm careful and wait for dark, I mean. It's buckskins and beard that mark me—and the Ovaro, who's gonna be boarded."

"Uh-huh, mebbe so. But Salt Lake City spreads out like a fat man's ass. We gonna patrol the whole place?"

"Nix on that," Fargo said. "Too many constables and roundsmen—fear of Indians. And they set loose packs of dogs at night, too. They might raise a ruckus and get us nabbed."

Old Billy sputtered drily when he tried again to spit. "Christ, I'm spittin' cotton. And we gotta cross this big son of a bitch alla way to Sacramento."

Even the Trailsman, who cheerfully accepted most terrain the West set before him, felt humbled and daunted in the Great Salt. The vast desert plain stretched between scarred ranges of sterile mountains. The wind-driven grit stung like buckshot, and a blazing yellow sun was stuck high in the sky as if pegged there. Alkali dust hung curtain-thick in the air, the searing sunlight turning it into a blinding white haze.

"What I think we should do," Fargo said, picking up the conversational thread from earlier, "is concentrate on the outlying places, including Mormon Station. He'll be got up to look like me, and with that pinto he's riding he'd be a double-barreled fool to ride into the city."

"I still say he's a haint," Old Billy insisted.

"Sell your ass. How would a ghost hold a Henry rifle? Or, for that matter, wear buckskins?"

"Hell, Fargo, you yourself said he just disappeared today. And there wa'n no horse."

"A Comanche can sneak in and out of a rolling wagon without being seen. And he left the horse hidden for obvious reasons."

"Stuff," Old Billy protested. "How in blue blazes could he know we was coming up to them dunes?"

"He didn't, you mule-headed fool. Likely he was up there to get the lay of the land below, see how the wind sets. Anyway, I'd guess he'll wait until dark. With luck we can pop him over before he strikes again. Say, what's this?"

Fargo had just spotted a ramshackle structure straight

ahead, obscured by blowing sand. Both men filled their hands and rode in slow. The weather-rawed shack was barely larger than a packing crate and showed no signs of life. He guessed it was an old sentry post—the history of Mormons in America had taught them extreme vigilance.

"Hallo, the shack!" Fargo called out.

"Hell, anybody inside that cracker box would roast to death," Old Billy scoffed.

Fargo nodded. "But look at that brush ramada in front. We can at least wait out of the sun."

He lit down and held the reins as, standing to one side, he kicked at the dilapidated plank door. It broke free of its dry-rotted leather hinges and fell onto the dirt inside. Squinting in the bright sunlight, Fargo made out a plank table, a nail keg, and trash heaped everywhere.

"It's got the smell of an outlaw hideout," he told Old Billy, "but nobody's been here in a coon's age."

There was a small apron of shade on the east side of the shack, so they tethered their mounts there and watered them out of the sun. Then the two men squatted under the ramada, grateful for a little relief.

"Ain't you been wondering," Old Billy said as they gnawed on strips of jerked buffalo, "who in Sam Hill is behind this outlaw Fargo? You think it's a gang or just one hombre?"

"Might as well ask me where lost years go. The only evidence we've got points to one man."

"Ain't no use," Billy added, "to wunner who might hate you. That's like askin' if an old hound has fleas."

Fargo grinned. "Sing it, brother. I keep running all the hard cases through my mind, but I can't put one to the top of the heap. I've killed plenty of the men I've locked horns with, and sent plenty more to prison. Whoever it is ain't content to see me pushing daisies. He wants to see me get one helluva comeuppance—he means to change my reputation forever and see me busting rocks in a Mormon prison before I swing."

Old Billy grunted, picking at his teeth with a horseshoe nail. "I'll give it to you straight-arrow, Fargo—he's damn close to gettin' what he wants."

"No, he's not," Fargo said with conviction. "I'll kill him and the truth will all come out in the wash."

The sun was still a crimson afterthought on the western horizon when Fargo and Old Billy, keeping a wary eye out, trotted their mounts into Salt Lake City. The wide, creosote-oiled streets of this plain and simple God-fearing town were mostly deserted—a rollicking nightlife was not characteristic of Mormon culture. It made Fargo feel like a naked target.

Here and there he spotted rustic outlanders, some sporting coyote-skin caps, prowling the streets under the watchful eye of civil but vigilant soldiers. Old Billy kept the Ovaro on the shadowy side of the street.

"Belly of the beast," Old Billy muttered. "I'll breathe a mite easier when we get shed of these mounts for a spell."

"Hold your whist, old son. Mica's place is dead ahead."

The Ovaro, always a little flighty when riding into a settlement, snorted and pricked up his ears at Fargo's words. Of all the liverymen Fargo had encountered in his wanderings, none knew or appreciated horses more than Mica.

Fargo tugged rein and they trotted through the pole gate of a thriving livery on the western outskirts of town. In the light of a lantern they spotted a gaunt and gnarled old man who looked to be straight out of Genesis. He was in the paddock working a blindfolded coyote dun on a breaking pole and controlling it with apparent ease.

"Micajah," Fargo called out. "Mica Jones. Got room to board two more horses?"

The old hostler glanced toward them, squinting in the weak light. He tried to place the smooth-shaven Fargo then dismissed him as an outlander.

"Mister," he said to Billy, "air ye daft? I know that horse. He can stop on a quarter and give you fifteen cents in change. But your life ain't worth a busted trace chain if Skye Fargo catches you on it—that's his Ovaro."

"Hell, I killed Fargo," Old Billy boasted. "Bashed his brains out with a tent stake."

Mica shook with laughter. "By grab, that's a corker. You ain't man enough to whip Fargo's shadow."

Old Billy bristled like a feist. "Look here, dad. Don't presume on them gray hairs. I don't cotton to that frosty lip of yours."

"Speakin' of lip," Mica retorted, "you got enough for two mouths."

"Don't listen to this chucklehead," Fargo told the livery-man as he swung down and dropped the Appaloosa's bridle, letting Billy's mount drink from a stone watering trough. "I'm still above the ground, Mica. That's my Ovaro, all right."

"Dang garn it, Fargo, I thought I recollected your voice. Ain't seen you since that fine animal of yours won the big horse race three years ago. Folks around here call him the Broken Drum—can't be beat."

"Right now," Fargo lamented, "he can't even be rode—not by me."

"Aye, I been hearing all the claptrap about you going on a woman-killing spree."

"Do they credit the story here in Salt Lake?"

"Only the fools, but that's a big enough majority in any town, eh? You best watch your ampersand—the big bugs in the Territorial Commission has put up a thousand-dollar reward for your capture. For that kind of legem pone a man don't *care* if you're innocent."

"A thousand dollars?" Old Billy whistled. "Fargo, put your damn hands up."

Fargo didn't bother to grin. Where gold and Old Billy were in the mix, loyalty was a dicey notion.

"You needn't cut capers," Mica told Billy, "they got a kill-or-capture order on you. That is, if you're knowed as Old Billy."

Now Fargo did grin. "He is."

The Indian fighter glowered at his companion. "Fargo, you double-poxed hound! Easy wages, you told me! Hell and furies, you are one son of trouble."

Mica chuckled as he led them inside the livery and produced a jug of mash from beneath a pile of straw in the first stall.

"Obliged," Billy said as he set it on his shoulder.

"Finest horse I ever seen," Mica said with deep respect, moving slowly around the Ovaro and studying him with an expert eye. "Never felt a breaking saddle. None of that choking nor water-starving nor wire bits to slice his mouth when he rebelled. And no cutting—a gelded horse will always lose bottom in a hard run on account he's spirit-broke."

"Why, hell yes," Old Billy agreed, wiping his mouth on his sleeve. "If some bastard lopped your nuts off, ain't likely you'd be dancing a jig. But say, old-timer, that Appaloosa of mine has got plenty of bottom for a gelding."

"Good breed," Mica agreed, handing the jug to Fargo. "Say, Trailsman, ain't you paring the cheese mighty close to the rind? Soldiers and lawmen are combing this neck of the Utah Territory looking for you and your pard here."

"Yeah, I'm in the grizzly's den," Fargo replied as he stripped the saddle, blanket, and pad from the Ovaro. "Soldiers, huh? How many?"

"Only a squad right now under your old friend Captain Lee. Utes got most of the rest tied up in the Wasatch."

Fargo welcomed the news. Captain Saunders Lee, a Mormon convert from the U.S. Army, had fought beside Fargo here in Deseret to break up a ring of whiskey peddlers selling to Indians. Fargo still intended to avoid soldiers, but if he had to fall into their net, he'd prefer Lee to be in charge.

"It ain't just soldiers and lawmen asking about you," Mica added. He was already working the Ovaro's sore shoulder muscles with gnarled but deft hands.

Fargo, who was heading to the tack room with his saddle and bridle, stopped and turned around. "Mind chewing that a little finer?"

"Yestiddy and today this shifty little fox-faced fellow come in. Sneaky-looking little bastard—never seen him afore in my life. He ain't no Mormon and sure odds he was never Bible raised. He didn't ask for you by name. Wanted to know if two fellows was boarding horses here—a black-and-white pinto stallion and an Appaloosa."

"Think he mighta been a law dog?" Fargo asked.

Mica shrugged. "Don't seem likely. Anyhow he didn't flash no tin star. Could be a bounty hunter—they ain't too savory looking."

"Bastard might come back," Old Billy fretted, "and spot our mounts."

"Mebbe," Mica agreed, "but the second time he come I told him I only board horses of Mormons I know."

"A fox-faced fellow," Fargo repeated, brow creased in concentration. "You recall anything else about him?"

Mica paused in his labors, thinking. "His eyes. They kept shifting around like a man with enemies to all sides. Never once looked me in the eye. And he carried one a them fat-bladed Spanish dags tucked into a red sash."

Enlightenment transformed Fargo's face. "Christ! That shifty bastard would be Orrin Trapp."

Old Billy tossed his saddle on a wooden rack and turned to look at Fargo. "So you know him?"

"Know him, and hauled him to trial for the murder of a federal paymaster in west Texas. Him and two others in the gang—Butch Landry and Harlan Perry. I killed Landry's kid brother, Ralston, in a shootout down in the Big Bend country. Landry was the leader of the gang."

"Was they convicted?"

"Hard labor for life at the federal prison in Sedalia, Missouri. Obviously they pulled a bust-out."

"Yeah," Old Billy said, "and obviously they mean to play turnabout on you. That's why the trouble didn't commence until we hit Utah. They want you to taste the joys of prison before you piss down your leg at the end of a rope."

Mica's face, wrinkled as an old apple core, eased into a grin. "Whatever happens to Fargo, Billy, will happen to you."

Fargo spoke up before Billy could retort. "Billy, it all fits, all right, except for one thing. Who's playing Fargo? Trapp is a runt, Butch is too stocky, and Perry is way too big. It has to be the same jasper who played Dr. Jacoby and killed Louise Tipton in Echo Canyon. He's built like me, so they've put a fourth man on the payroll."

"I know you figure the Lord threw away the mold when he made you," Old Billy barbed, "but every swinging dick has a look-alike somewheres. They musta found yours."

Fargo conceded this with a nod. "Well, thanks to Mica, we know who it is that's been on us like ugly on a buzzard— or anyhow, who's behind it. And we know they're here in Salt Lake City."

"It's a damn mare's nest," Old Billy said, rubbing his chin. "Mighty dangersome. So far, these three killers you hauled in don't seem to be taking a hand in it. More like, they're just trailing along to watch the fun."

"The way you say. They're fugitives and need to lay low.

But that fourth jackal, the one who tossed lead at us out at the dunes trying to snuff your wick, is staying plenty busy. And while we're standing here flapping our gums, he's likely painting the landscape red again."

He fell silent, not wanting the old man to be incriminated by hearing any plans.

"Mica," he said, turning to the hostler, "you got two good horses to let?"

"I got a black and a blood bay you can use—won't show in the dark."

Fargo nodded. "Good. And remember, if anything goes wrong, and me and Billy get the net tossed around us, you didn't recognize me without my beard and buckskins. I'm Frank Scully and this is Jim Lawson. That's all you know."

"Be pretty hard to say I missed that half-purple face of Billy's. Looks like somebody tossed a pot of ink into his face."

"Purple's the color of royalty," Old Billy fired back.

"Come on, King William," Fargo cut in. "Let's tack these new horses and survey your kingdom."

A voice reached... It was a soft, feminine voice humming.

"Listen to the M... me Bird," heard those th... stoptions: ...tion, Deets para... watch! Bathe in the nearby... soon g... ...othing about...   Somee...

14

James "Deets" Gramlich shared at least one thing in common with the man he was working hard to ruin: He never waded in until he knew how deep the water was. He had carefully scouted the area around Mormon Station, and he knew its strictly regimented routine.

His original plan was to leave the Fargo disguise off and make a tryst with a Mormon girl he knew when she lived in San Bernardino, showing up as Fargo to rape and cut her. But he hadn't caught sight of her all day and suspected the willful gal had run off with some gentile. Then he discovered something better.

At the far end of the melon fields an underground spring formed a natural bathing pool the size of a large room. And clearly the modest Mormons had reserved it for women only: Female after female had walked out from the settlement carrying soap and a towel with no men—except him—anywhere in sight.

Low-crawling through the melons just after sundown, he was now hidden within only twenty feet of the pool. The full moon and star-shot sky made the water gleam like liquid silver, and he watched a middle-aged matron scrub herself off. Nice dugs, he thought idly, but too much belly. Since he intended to relieve the pressure in his loins before he put the Arkansas toothpick to work, he might as well take a chance and see if something younger came along.

The woman finished, splashed onto dry ground, and toweled off. When she left, Deets was alone with the singsong cadence of insects and the rustle of wind in the huge melon patch. He could just make out the impressive silhouettes of the mountains ringing the valley.

A voice reached his ears: a soft, feminine voice humming "Listen to the Mocking Bird." Heart thudding with anticipation, Deets pressed himself flatter in the warm dirt. Soon a woman glided into view in the moonlight, a young woman with a long blond braid down the center of her back.

He watched her remove a frumpy shirtwaist and a long calico skirt, letting them fall in a puddle around her feet. In a moment she had shimmied out of a petticoat and chemise, then stepped out of her pantaloons to stand naked in the moonlight.

Deets forgot to breathe, the sight was so stunning. Her ass, firm and high-split, gleamed like polished ivory. She turned sideways to pick up her knot of soap and he saw taut breasts with hard, pointing nipples.

This, he realized, was an embarrassment of riches. Even Belle Lajeunesse, the San Francisco actress he had cut to bloody streamers, had not looked this fetching. Better, the outrage this beauty's attack would foment must surely turn all of Utah against Skye Fargo. And then Deets would work the final part of his plan—a plan completely at odds with what Butch Landry was paying him to do.

The girl gingerly tested the water with one dainty foot, and Deets sprang into action.

Mounted on a new horse, Fargo breathed a bit easier. The two horsebackers rode right past a blue-helmeted roundsman who only nodded at them cordially.

"So what's the big idea?" Old Billy asked as they rode down Tabernacle Street. "Now we know them three owl-hoots are here in town, why'n't we ride out to the outlander camps and roust them? Like you just said, they're fugitives. We can run them in and lay out the story for the law dogs."

Fargo shook his head. "Old son, if I was ever tempted. Sure, they're fugitives and the Mormons will likely have dodgers on them. But that bunch aren't about to admit this Skye Fargo plan. And we'd just be pinched along with 'em."

Old Billy mulled that and nodded. "A-huh. We'd just be looking for our own graves."

"Our clue is that ambush earlier at the salt dunes north of town," Fargo said. "The killer wouldn't be hanging around there unless he had his eye on Mormon Station. It's just a roll of the dice, but we can't be everywhere at once. Let's dust our hocks toward the north valley."

"I'm with you till the wheels fall off," Old Billy shot back. "But speakin' of them salt dunes—that shit-eating polecat had to get a good gander at you, right?"

Fargo had been thinking about that himself and knew where this trail was headed. "You're thinking that by now he knows I've shaved my beard and chucked my buckskins?"

"Hell yes. Might be he knew it before he seen you. Them jackleg lawmen at Junebug Kellar's place seen you, too. Good chance this bastard has got hisself shaved and into different duds. It's the Ovaro that will sink you—you can't shave a horse's markings."

"Here's the way I see it," Fargo replied. "Right now we're neither up the well nor down. Whatever this son of a bitch is doing with fake beards is nothing to the matter. What *does* matter is that I get his life over, the quicker the better. All the evidence of beards and such will be on him—and the best evidence will be his horse. So let's knock him out from under his hat."

"By the horn spoons!" Billy exclaimed. "Let's put your twin brother to work shovelin' coal in hell!"

Salt Lake City strictly enforced the law against "speedy and reckless riding" in the city streets. Impatient at the delay, Fargo nudged the coal black gelding up to a fast trot and held him at that pace. The horse was a typical Micajah Jones mount: well-trained and spirited. Like Fargo, it was eager to run but did not fight the restraint of the reins.

The moment they reached the outskirts of the settlement, Fargo thumped its flanks with his boot heels and the black surged forward. It was no Ovaro—few horses were—but the rataplan of hoofbeats increased through a canter and a lope to a strong gallop.

The valley road was wide and well graded, and in the sterling moonlight visibility was excellent. Fargo decided against riding directly into the double row of cabins—an attack there by his deadly look-alike seemed too risky. He would need to catch his victim at a distance from the cabins, and only two reasons would call a Mormon woman out at night: a "necessary trip" to the outlying jakes or a visit to the bathing pool at the edge of the fields. Fargo had learned about the pool during his first visit to the Salt Lake Valley, when he was sternly warned to avoid it by a Mormon elder who knew his reputation for frolics with the ladies.

Soon the lights from Mormon Station hove into view, twinkling like fireflies. Fargo pulled back on the reins. Old Billy reined in beside him. "What's on the spit?"

Fargo pointed left. "We're going to ride through the field now, but make sure you stay between the rows—trampling crops is a felony around here. See the outline of those trees down there? That's a bathing pool reserved for women."

Old Billy snorted. "Fargo, you pick queerlike times to go in rut."

"Sell your ass, you damn fool. That's the best place for the killer to strike. By strict Mormon law, men can't go near that spot, so our boy has got easy pickings."

Old Billy liked the sound of this. "If he's there we'll send him over the mountains. Happens he ain't, might see some titties and it won't cost me nothing."

Fargo loosed a long, fuming sigh and shook his head. "Look, just ride in slow, and make sure your bit ring doesn't jangle. About fifty feet or so away we'll dismount and hobble our horses. We'll hoof it in from there, but do *not* spy on the women. We're only watching for our killer."

"Don't spy my lily-white ass," Old Billy fumed as they entered a big melon field. "Fargo, I'll look away if it's some big fat breed cow on the yonder side of fifty with dugs trailing on the ground. But happens I spot a pert set of puffy loaves on a young gal, goddamn my eyes if I ain't lookin'! And you will too, you pussy hound."

Fargo said nothing, for of course it was true.

Goosebumps chilled her skin as Katy Emerson waded into the pool, but she liked bathing late. For one thing it was refreshing after the day's furnace heat. For another, she sought the privacy. The other women stared at her naked form with envy and resentment, as if she, and not the Good Lord, had made her body this way.

When the water was up to her hips she unbraided her long

113

golden hair and dipped in over her head, gasping as she broke the surface again. She was still wiping the water from her eyes when a low male voice behind her announced, "Oh, muffin, we're *both* going to enjoy this."

In the moments of shocked silence following this, the man behind her wrapped a cloth over her mouth and quickly knotted it. She whirled to confront her attacker. In the generous moon wash she glimpsed a handsome, smooth-shaven face sporting a twisted smile. The blade of a long, thin knife glinted cruelly in the moonlight.

"Yes," he assured her, "it's Skye Fargo without his beard. Now it won't burn when I rub my face in those succulent tits. Best melons in the field."

She reached for the gag, but he suddenly threw a crashing right fist into her jaw and her knees buckled. He caught her and carried her to the grassy bank, laying her down and spreading her legs open. But in the time it took him to open his fly and lay his gun belt next to the Henry in the grass, her eyes fluttered open and she regained consciousness.

She managed only to begin a piercing scream before he cursed and slugged her again. Before he could either cut or rape her, however, the drumbeat of rapidly approaching hooves pushed him to the brink of panic.

The Mormon settlers could not have mounted and begun the chase in the short time since she screamed. That meant Skye Fargo was now bearing down on him like a Doomsday juggernaut!

His heart stomped violently against his ribs as he fumbled his trousers closed and shot to his feet. Repeating rifles opened up, bullets chunking into the cottonwood trees all around him—aimed deliberately high, he gratefully noted, to avoid hitting innocents. But in a few moments they'd be able to make him out in the moonlight, and Deets had heard that incredible story about Fargo shooting a hawk on the wing in Echo Canyon.

He buckled on his gun belt—black leather just like Fargo's—and snatched up the Henry from the ground. Deets could not boast the shooting prowess of Fargo, but he had spent plenty of time practicing with the Henry. He knelt behind a gnarled cottonwood and threw the butt-plate into his shoulder. He could see the two horsebackers now, dark shadows gliding across the face of the moon, and he opened fire, levering rapidly to lay down a withering field of fire.

It must have been accurate, he realized, because both men leaped from their horses and went to ground. Deets had left the pinto behind a granary about a quarter mile beyond the bathing pool. He took advantage of the hiatus in their charge and bolted into the night, leaving the stunning Mormon woman naked and unconscious in the grass.

Fargo rose to his knees in the melon field, the long barrel of his Henry still emitting curls of smoke.

"He decided to rabbit," he told Old Billy. "I saw a shadow round the pool. C'mon, let's tote up the butcher's bill."

Both men stepped up into leather and raced their steeds toward the end of the field. Fargo heard shouts behind them and knew more trouble was coming—the Mormons had heard the gunplay and would know that one of their womenfolk was in trouble.

They reined in at the edge of the moon-gleaming pool and immediately spotted the pale beauty in the grass.

"Christ on a mule, he killed her," Old Billy fretted as they lit down. "Fargo, we best rabbit ourselves afore them Saints get here. You *know* what them hell-and-brimstone Mormons will do to two gentiles what killed one a their women—and *look* at her, man! By the twin balls of Saint Peter she's a beauty!"

"She's some pumpkins," Fargo agreed, kneeling beside her. "But she ain't dead—and no cuts. Just a bruise making up on her jaw. Old son, we mighta got here in the nick of time."

A growing hubbub was heading toward them across the field, a confusion of shouting male voices. Several torches flickered in the darkness, but Fargo was grateful they had left their horses grazing.

"Damn it, Fargo, quit ogling her catheads and let's pull foot. That mob is closing in on us."

"Stay frosty, Indian fighter," Fargo replied, dipping his hat into the pool and splashing cold water on the girl.

Her eyes trembled open, and for at least ten seconds she

stared into Fargo's face without comprehension. Then, as memory returned, her pretty face contorted into a mask of abject fear.

"You!" she said, trying to make herself smaller in the grass. "No, don't touch me!"

She sucked in a huge breath and screamed so loud the sound pierced Fargo's ears like jagged shards of glass. It was like a warning siren to the advancing Mormons—a crackling volley of gunshots opened up, deadly lead making the air hum.

"Stupid bastards," Fargo muttered even as a round tugged at his shirt passing through. "They'll kill her."

"Stay flat!" Fargo ordered her even as he and Old Billy leaped for their horses.

"Let's get off to the flanks," Fargo said as he leaped onto the rented mount, wishing it was the Ovaro. "Then toss some snap-shots into the air so those damn turnip-heads will stop firing toward the girl. Let's rendezvous at that desert shack we found earlier."

Once again, Fargo thought grimly, he had to let that stinking sage rat scurry to safety. And whether or not that unfortunate beauty had been raped tonight, Skye Fargo would be accused of a heinous attack on an innocent woman.

But as he thumped the gelding's ribs with his heels and they vaulted forward, angry bullets still seeking his vitals, Fargo's lips formed a grim, determined slit. No posse would corral this killer, no judge decide his fate. He had raped, wounded, and murdered women in the name of Skye Fargo, and his only refuge would be in the hottest pit of hell.

15

Captain Saunders Lee unsnapped the brim of his cavalry hat
to provide a little more shade for his sunburned face. Each
breath of the desert air was like molten glass, and sweat
evaporated the moment it appeared.

"Sergeant Shoemaker," he called to the NCO behind him,
"we'll walk the horses for thirty minutes to spell them."

"Yessir!"

"And call in the flankers. There's a band of Paiutes down
from the Humboldt River, and I'd rather have every man
here in the main gather. Nobody can sneak up on us in this
country."

The burly sergeant barked out the order and the squad of
twelve Mormon soldiers dismounted, taking their horses by
the reins to lead them. Saunders, leading his roan, glanced
all around this parched corner of the Great Salt Desert, his
eyes trembling and watering. This salt desert hardpan produced a glare that could drive animals and humans mad.
Back east Salt Lake City was being called the "Halfway
House" between the Missouri River and the Pacific Ocean.

But all he'd found, so far, was a harsh, unforgiving land
of tarantulas, centipedes, and scorpions. In this desolate salt-
desert waste, no joyous birds celebrated sunup. It was an arid
land of *borrasca*, barren rock. It was terrain so hostile that
even the mission padres gave it wide berth. The Great Basin
was devoid of humanity except for a few nomadic braves,
mostly Utes and a few Paiutes or Shoshonis.

He became aware that Sergeant Shoemaker had edged up
beside him.

"Sir, permission to speak freely?"

Saunders' weather-creased face was split by a grin. "Of course. What's on your mind besides your hat?"

"It's this godless outlander, Skye Fargo. Is it true you and him were friends once?"

"Still are for aught I know. Oh, we weren't joined at the hip or anything like that, but, yes, we were friends."

Shoemaker's big, bluff face molded into a frown. "Still are even after he tried to . . . outrage Katy Emerson?"

"Look, Shoemaker, Skye Fargo has 'outraged' plenty of women, all right, but not in the sense you mean. Fargo can have his pick of any willing women, and when the women see him, an awful lot of them become willing."

"Even Mormon women?"

"They're women too, aren't they?"

Shoemaker took the reins under one arm and pulled the makings from his tunic, building himself a cigarette. He struck a lucifer to life with his thumb and leaned into the flame.

"Well, sir, you talk Fargo up pretty high, and I'm one for respecting your view of it. But when the Territorial Commission puts out a kill-or-capture order on a man, they must have some strong evidence."

Saunders nodded. "True, but evidence can be strong and still not be true. And get this straight: We're going to *capture* Fargo, not kill him. We serve Mormon law, not the Territorial Commission."

"You really think we'll find him out in this god-forgotten desert?"

"You can't know with Fargo. He likes to keep his adversaries surprised, mystified, and confused. But when he's under the gun like he is now, he tends to lay low in the worst possible terrain. And being a veteran scout, he prefers open country when he's being pursued—his eyes are so sharp he can see into the middle of next week."

Shoemaker blew a series of perfect smoke rings. "Well, the crimes he's been accused of was bad enough when it was just gentile women. Now they're saying he attacked Katy Emerson, the prettiest girl in Deseret. And speaking of Mormon law—flight is evidence of guilt. It won't be easy, sir, to control the men—they got blood in their eyes."

Saunders slanted a glance toward his subordinate. "Are you hinting at rebellion in the ranks, Sergeant?"

Shoemaker's face became a blank slate. "No, sir. I believe in subordination as the proper friend of mankind—that's why I'm in the army. So far this Trailsman has foxed us. But I just fear the men might slip their traces if we spot Fargo."

Saunders bit back his first reply. Instead he said, "Shoemaker, aren't you forgetting something?"

"Sir?"

"You heard the description of events from Mormon Station. There was a gun battle before our people even responded. Yet, no Saint has come forward to say he was in that battle. Clearly, whoever attacked Katy Emerson was himself attacked."

"I never really thought of that. But now you mention it . . ."

"That's not all," Saunders said. "Katy said the same man who appeared to have attacked her also revived her with water and then told her to stay down while the bullets were whizzing in. She thought his shirt was different, too. I'd say that suggests that somebody is passing himself off as Fargo."

Shoemaker flipped his butt away in a wide arc. He thought about the captain's last remarks as he played with his left earlobe. His face was powdered white from the gritty alkali soil.

"You may have a point there, sir. After all, we know from the report at Echo Canyon that Fargo has got shed of his buckskins. If Katy wasn't just roiled in her head, and there was two men, neither one wore buckskins. That's a mite curious."

"A mite," Saunders agreed as, eyes closed to mere slits against a merciless sun, he studied the bleak terrain around him and hoped he wouldn't spot one damn sign of Skye Fargo.

After escaping from the crowd at Mormon Station, Fargo and Old Billy Williams took refuge in the deserted shack west of Salt Lake City. They rolled out of their blankets early enough to make a small fire before the smoke would show. Fargo boiled a handful of coffee beans while scanning the flat horizon to the north.

"Soldiers are patrolling about ten miles out," he reported after a copper-colored sun seemed to just suddenly appear in the sky.

"How can you tell it's soldiers?" Old Billy grumped. "Dust puffs is dust puffs. Could be featherheads or a freight caravan."

"Give this infant a dug," Fargo shot back. "They call you an Indian fighter? You know Indians never ride in tight formations—they scatter to hell and gone and leave a wide dust pattern. A freight caravan moves so slow it hardly kicks up any dust. These puffs are tight and orderly—soldiers."

"Looking for us, likely, after that brouhaha last night."

Fargo nodded. "Likely."

Old Billy squatted on his heels outside the shack and tried to spit into the sand. "Fargo, you are so goldang evil that Satan calls you sir. I signed on to help site through some line stations. Now here I am, wanted by the hull damn Mormon nation. Any unlucky son of a bitch who throws in with you might as well get measured for a coffin."

Fargo dismissed this with a wave of his hand. "The ass waggeth his ears. I never forced you to put your oar in my boat, you greedy piker. The moment you heard the pay was five dollars a day you had gold lust in your eyes."

Old Billy grunted but said nothing—every word was true.

"Gold lust," Fargo repeated, "and yet you won't even plank a dime for a cold beer. Billy, men like us can go under at any moment. Why would you want to die with a pile of unspent money for your killer to take? Old son, that gold won't spend in heaven *or* hell. Enjoy it while you can."

"Stow the preaching, Reverend Fargo, and keep your nose out of the pie. What I do with my money ain't none of your picnic."

Old Billy poured himself a cup of coffee, blew on it to cool it, then took a loud sip. He spat it out. "Tarnal hell, Fargo! A man could cut a plug off this coffee."

"Well, hell yes. Good coffee's not ready until it'll float a horseshoe. We're low on rations, and this is at least something to chew on."

"Bust a tooth on, you mean."

But Old Billy wasn't really listening for a retort. His purple-stained, homely face was lost in reflection. "Speaking of rations—this murdering twin of yours is being kept alive by somebody. You figure it's that gang you mentioned?"

"Butch Landry, Orrin Trapp, and Harlan Perry. Sure as cats fighting it has to be them. We know they're somewhere around Salt Lake City. The way he has to keep moving, he needs supplies and such provided."

"I'll give him this much," Old Billy said. "The horn-toad bastard is stubborn as a government mule. He don't plan to give over."

"The way you say. But what you just mentioned—about who's supplying him. It ain't just food and ammo they're giving him—it's money, plenty of it. Likely from that payroll heist that was never recovered. And if we can't lop off the head of the snake, maybe we can chop off the tail."

Old Billy nodded. "You're thinking them three sewer rats are staying in the outlander camps at the edge of town?"

"Where else? It's damn near impossible for a gentile to rent a place in the city unless he knows a Mormon. And seeing as how they're fugitives, they can't roost in the open desert. Your typical criminal seeks towns and would starve without stores."

"Uh-huh, but *we're* fugitives, too. After that shooting fray last night, we'd be bigger fools than God made us if we go back into the city."

Fargo shook his head. "Nah. Nobody saw our mounts. And the girl didn't see you—only me. Both of me. We'll go in after dark."

Old Billy brightened up. "Hell yes! We'll powder-burn all three of them and take off like dogs with our asses afire! Fargo, you've set my blood singing!"

"Nix on that, you numbskull. We want them alive to prove who hired the Fargo look-alike. We got to clear our names. Besides, Mormons don't look kindly upon vigilante justice. No, we're just going to locate them. Then we send the Salt Lake police an anonymous note telling them where three escaped killers can be found. That way, they'll be safely behind bars while we track down their hired jobber."

"And with them three pinched," Old Billy suggested, "good chance he won't *be* their jobber no more."

Fargo nodded. He shucked out his Colt and rolled the wheel against his palm to check the action. This hard-blown desert grit was tough on the workings of a firearm.

"Our trail will eventually cross his," he said in a calm but determined voice. "So far his clover has been deep, but luck only lasts a lifetime if a man dies young."

At the grainy twilight hour Fargo liked to call "between dog and wolf," two riders appeared out of the desert and rode into the outskirts of Salt Lake City. Coal-oil streetlamps burned at every corner, casting lurid shadows and weak penumbras of oily yellow light. Fargo intended to visit Mica at the livery before searching the outlander camps.

As always the streets were well guarded. As Fargo and Old Billy trotted their rented mounts down wide Commerce Street, an armed roundsman barked out from the rammed-earth sidewalk: "You two men! Halt and be identified!"

"Kill him?" Old Billy muttered.

"Hold off. If we have to dust quick, wrap him up with your bolos. Remember our new names."

Both men hauled back on the reins and the roundsman, an old mule-ear rifle trained on them, walked out into the street. "Who are you?" he demanded, squinting as he peered at their faces in the scant light.

Fargo had selected new names for them, realizing the summer names given at Echo Canyon might be known here.

"I'm Neal Bryce," Fargo replied, "and this is my partner Del Baptiste."

"Partner?"

"We're wolfers and long-fur trappers. Headed out to California. We hear the farmers around San Bernardino are losing livestock to wolf packs. Thought we'd see if we could hire out."

The guard nodded. San Bernardino was the only Mormon settlement outside of Utah, and wolves were indeed plaguing the region.

The guard looked at Old Billy. "Where do you gents hail from?"

"Missouri," Old Billy answered, and Fargo immediately winced. Back in the 1840s, eastern Missouri had been the scene of some of the worst massacres of Mormons—the same bloody attacks that had forced the Mormon exodus to Deseret.

"West Missouri," Fargo hastily amended. "We had to skedaddle because of the damn Border Ruffians. Anybody who isn't pro-slaver is either run out or killed."

The guard walked around their horses and took a closer look at their weapons. "You men seem well-armed. Is that a Henry rifle?" he asked Old Billy, peering at his scabbard.

"Yep. Load it on Sunday and fire it all week."

"Were you firing it last night at Mormon Station?"

Fargo didn't like the turn this trail was taking. Discreetly, he knocked the riding thong off the hammer of his Colt.

"Never heard of Mormon Station," he replied calmly. "This is our first time in the Utah Territory."

"Why would you be riding into Salt Lake City after sunset? This is a God-fearing settlement where families are at home after dark. We have no saloons, no women of loose morals, and no gambling houses. As you rode in you must have seen the posted notice saying all that."

The roundsman's voice had tightened with suspicion. Fargo decided to roll the dice. "Sure, we saw it. But I was hoping to say a quick hello to my cousin."

"You have a Mormon cousin?"

"Well, he is now—he's a convert from the Methodist religion. His name is Saunders Lee."

"Saunders—you're Captain Lee's cousin?"

"My mother is his aunt. Me and Saunders both served in the U.S. Army before he converted. Fought Sioux and Cheyenne out in the western Nebraska Territory. He met a pretty little Mormon gal named Dora Stratton—pretty as four aces. If he's still above the ground, I expect he's married her by now."

The sentry's tone altered remarkably. "He's still alive, friend, and he did indeed marry Dora. They have their first young'un on the way. Well, I'll be dinged! Captain Lee's cousin. You'll be able to say howdy to Dora, all right, but I'm afraid Saunders is on patrol in the desert west of town. Won't likely return for a few more days. He's searching for a fugitive named Skye Fargo."

"Fargo?" repeated Old Billy. "I've heard of that hard case. Raping and killing women . . . He needs to be buried naked in an anthill."

"If he's guilty," the sentry said. "I don't believe he is. Fargo is a hard man, and he's a cold killer when he has to be. But he's straight grain clear through."

Fargo could tell Old Billy didn't like this praise, but he wisely kept his lips sewed shut.

"Well, Neal," the sentry said to Fargo, "you'll find the Lee home at the corner of Tabernacle and Kirtland streets. The white cottage with gingerbread trim."

Fargo thanked him and the two riders gigged their mounts into motion.

"Straight grain clear through," Old Billy muttered. "Ain't *that* sweet lavender? Fargo, I seen you set fire to a cathouse in New Orleans. And what about that time you helped run wagon-yard whiskey to them miners in Silver City?"

"It was straight grain," Fargo quipped. "Clear through. Anyhow, never mind. We got bigger fish to fry. Quit jacking your jaws and keep a sharp eye out. As soon as we're clear of that roundsman, we'll ride to the livery."

"Hell, you said this Captain Lee is your chum. Why not visit his wife and leave a message for him?"

"He's a friend, not my mother," Fargo said. "He's a sworn officer in the Mormon Battalion, and he'll have to report that I'm here in the city. Besides, what would I say? This ain't a job to hire out—we'll do it ourselves."

"Right as rain," Old Billy conceded. "Even a fool can put his own pants on better than the guv'ment can do it for him."

A buggy with its top up against the dust rolled past them. They passed a harness shop, a mercantile, a cooperage with barrels stacked in pyramids out front. Fargo noticed a few new redbrick buildings since his last trip here, for the Saints had recently established a brick furnace. They passed a raw-lumber home with a dour-faced matron sweeping sand off her porch. She stared at both men and puckered her face as if she had just whiffed skunk.

"Goddamn my eyes," Old Billy muttered in his raspy voice, "that woman's ugly as proud flesh. You could toss her in a pond and skim ugly for a month."

When it was clear, Fargo reined toward the western outskirts of town and Mica's livery. Fargo was especially worried about the horses. If Landry's gang had discovered them, they could be waiting in ambush to kill Fargo and Old Billy when they rode in for them.

So he didn't ride in. Leaving Old Billy back in the shadow of a schoolhouse to hold both horses, he hoofed it in cautiously and entered the livery through the rear doors, his Colt cocked and to hand. He spotted Mica at a workbench in the middle of the barn, pounding caulks into horseshoes.

"Hey up, old-timer," he said as he stepped inside and leathered his shooter. "Any trouble since I left?"

"Not so's you'd notice," Mica replied without looking up.

Fargo stopped at the Ovaro's stall and the stallion nuzzled his shoulder in greeting. Fargo scratched his withers. "Don't fret, old campaigner, you'll soon be stretching those legs out good."

"Anybody come in today asking about these horses?" he queried Mica.

"Nary a soul. 'Pears to me that fox-faced outlander musta believed my lie about only boarding horses belongin' to Mormons. Just to be safe, I lock up good at bedtime and sleep down here in a stall. Any egg-sucking varmint who tries to get in will get a seat-load of double-aught buckshot for his trouble."

Fargo chuckled. "'Preciate you keeping a close eye on my horse, Mica. But these three thugs asking about him are poison—don't stick your neck out. They'd steal Tiny Tim's crutch."

Mica now looked up at Fargo, his face craggy as a walnut shell. "These three mean badgers are the ones that've framed you, eh? Made you out to be a rapist and murderer of wimmin?"

Fargo nodded. "I don't have any proof yet that you could hang on a nail. And they're the ones bankrolling the fourth man who's doing the dirt work."

Fargo turned to leave. Mica spoke up behind him. "I hope you mean to kill all four of 'em. Kill one fly, kill a million."

Fargo sent the old hostler an over-the-shoulder glance. "Damn straight I'm killing the dirt worker. He made it personal. As for the other three, Mica—the one thing they fear more than anything is Mormon law. They'll have to spend two years at hard labor before they stretch hemp. It's one thing to die—it's another to know exactly *when* you're going to die. Unless they force my hand, I won't do them the favor of killing them."

16

Skye Fargo and Old Billy Williams trotted their horses toward the outlander camps, swinging toward the center of the street when they approached corner street lanterns.

"How do we play this?" Old Billy spoke up above the clip-clop of shod hooves. "Them camps is crowded with well-heeled men, and most of 'em ain't exactly what you'd call familiar with opera houses and good grooming."

Fargo grinned at the irony. "Listen to this jay! Old son, I have never once known you to take a bath. The punk blowing off you could raise blood blisters on a new saddle."

Old Billy bristled and puffed out his chest. "I'll sink you, boy! Never mind giving me the rough side of your tongue—I said how do we play this? Fargo, every man in that camp is poor as Job's turkey, and they all know about the reward on our hides. A pair of hombres riding in after dark—hell, they'll be all over us like two-bit perfume."

"They're not all poor," Fargo reminded him. "The three we're after have money to throw at the birds. But, anyhow, you're right, Old Billy. This will be a tricky piece of work."

Fargo fell silent, turning the problem back and forth for a while.

"We won't ride in together," Fargo decided. "You'll tie off on the east side of the camp, me on the west. You know what these scrotes look like—it's chilly tonight, most of the campers will be sitting around fires. The first one of us to see them will shout out, 'Hey, Jimmy, where are you?' That will be the other man's signal to return to his horse and skedaddle. But don't forget—each camp spot has a numbered stake. Make sure you read it."

"I reckon that'll do," Old Billy agreed. "I can cipher numbers. You always was good at horseback thinking, Fargo."

"If either of us hears gunfire break out," Fargo added as an afterthought, "never mind the 'Hey, Jimmy' business—just light out."

They reached the outskirts of Salt Lake City. Dead ahead they could see scores of campfires sawing in the brisk night gusts.

Old Billy managed to spit. "These goldang Mormons. They ain't so bad as some make out, but they got no respect for the rights of the wandering man. It's just like in England—a man can't hunt good meat unless he's poaching on the estate of some rich toff."

Fargo nodded agreement. "When I first started yondering you never saw a no-trespassing sign anywhere west of the Mississippi. It looked just like it did when Meriwether Lewis and Bill Clark sighted through it fifty-some years ago. Son, there was room to swing a cat in! Still is, room aplenty, but you can see it coming from the east—a thundering herd of land hunters, railroad men, and hard-rock miners. These confounded 'sportsmen' are already killing off the buffalo. After this big war they say is coming, cattle empires will start in deep Texas and spread north like a pox. Saddle bums like us will have to stay on pikes and pay a toll to do it."

Old Billy stared hard at his friend. "God's nightgown! You're a perky son of a bitch, ain't you? Will our peckers fall off, too?"

A second later, however, his tone changed. "I know you're right, Skye—right as the mail. And speaking on that, ain't we part of the problem, too? Look at us—taking free and open land to locate line stations for the Pony."

"We are," Fargo admitted. "But I only took the job because I knew them line stations will be weed lots inside two years. Waddell and his pards know the Pony will go bust fast. They figure it'll cost twenty times more to deliver a letter than it costs the customer to mail it. Meantime, though, it's a terrific sensation all over the damn world and bringing freighting business in hand over fist."

Old Billy rubbed his jaw. "That's how them new 'businessmen' think—burn up a small pile of money to get a bigger one. Me, I pinch every Bungtown copper until it cries 'ouch!' "

"I hadn't noticed," Fargo said drily. "But never mind—it's time to split up before any of the campers notice us. Give me the Henry—I'm going to cache it. Take Patsy Plumb with you—only a fool would come against a Greener. I'll take your Spencer so nobody heists it. Keep your face turned away from the flames in case the word is out about your birthmark. Remember, if you spot them get the number of their camp and then raise the shout for Jimmy. *Don't* brace the sons of bitches."

"You done, schoolman?" Old Billy said sarcastically. "Hell, I ain't no soft brain."

"Luck," Fargo called out to him before tugging rein and heading around to the far side of the sprawling camp. He wrapped the black gelding's reins around a long hitching post. There was no graze available but a good number of horses were tethered within range of a long water trough.

There was only moonlight to reveal him, and just as Fargo lit down the wind blew a raft of clouds in front of it. He quickly crossed to the trough and slid his Henry under it. Then, Billy's Spencer carbine carried muzzle-down under his left arm, he entered the sprawling camp.

Countless campfires cast a lurid orange glow, illuminating men's faces like half-remembered dream images. Some had tents and Fargo even spotted a few wickiups made from bent branches. Most of these men were the dregs or the destitute of the Far West: prospectors gone bust in the California goldfields, denizens of the owlhoot trail, down-at-the-heels laborers who went broke before they could reach Sacramento or San Francisco.

And every damn one of them, Fargo reminded himself, would have a new start in life if they captured or killed Skye Fargo, Utah's most wanted man.

Men were wandering aimlessly around, bored or lonely and looking to join in a campfire conversation. This made Fargo feel less conspicuous, especially as he stayed in the shape-shifting shadows. Any one of those wandering men might be a Mormon guard.

". . . no damn right to tax the meat we eat!" a rusty voice

fumed as Fargo passed a campfire. "We whipped John Bull for taxing our damn tea! The hell's next—a tax every time we take a piss?"

The speaker looked up at Fargo as he passed, watching him from a slanted glance. "How 'bout you, stranger?" he called out. "You support this Congress?"

"Add a politician to a nail," Fargo replied, "and you'll have a nail."

The men ringed around the fire broke into raucous laughter and Fargo passed safely by. Just ahead he saw a kid carrying a water yoke, full pails at either end. Fargo caught up to him.

"Maybe you can help me, son," he greeted the kid. "I got three cousins somewhere in camp but don't know the number of their spot. One looks like a bulldog, another's got a face like a fox, and the third one is big enough to fight cougars with a shoe."

"Sir, I can't read numbers," the kid replied. "But you'll find them three at the end of the second row—the end closest to town."

Fargo thanked the kid and slipped him two bits. He angled over to the second row and headed toward the end. He spotted the last fire and three figures seated around it. Fargo loosened his Colt in its holster and eased into the shadows behind them. He was stealing closer when cold steel pressed into the back of his neck.

"The hell you think you're doin', mister?" a gritty voice challenged him. Fargo turned slowly around and the scant light revealed a doltish-looking, slope-shouldered man. "Make any sudden moves and I'll put moonlight through you."

"The hell's your dicker?" Fargo demanded, doubting that such a slovenly looking man was a Mormon guard. "These are public camps, ain't they?"

"I want your opinion I'll beat it out of you. I heard you ask that kid about your three 'cousins.' Now I see you sneakin' up on 'em like a murderin' redskin. What, you a bounty hunter? Drop that carbine and ease your short gun out with two fingers."

Fargo cursed the luck. He was confident that he could draw steel and kill this man in a heartbeat. And usually, on the frontier, nobody asked any questions if the bullet hole was in front. But he was on the threshold of verifying where the Butch Landry gang was, and gunplay now would alert them before he learned that site number.

This was a situation invented for the silent "buffalo" developed by Western lawmen. His right arm moving like a piston, Fargo drew his Colt and in one smooth, fluid movement brought the barrel down hard on the top of the bullyboy's skull. He folded to the ground like an empty sack.

But disaster struck. When he hit the ground his primed and loaded rifle, a Sharp's Big Fifty firing a huge one-ounce ball, went off with a roar like a Spanish one-pounder. It was aimed straight at the last campfire and Fargo heard a sickening sound like a hammer hitting a watermelon. He glanced over just in time to see a huge man—Harlan Perry, he guessed—topple dead to the ground with half his head a crumpled, pulpy mess.

Clearly the gang had been nerved for attack, and the two survivors wasted no time opening up in Fargo's direction. Bullets thickened the air all around him, making snapping sounds as they whizzed past his head. Fargo debated laying down some fire to cover his retreat but realized he'd never make it out of this heavily armed camp if he wasted even a precious second.

His long legs carried him full tilt in the direction of his horse, Fargo's elbows pumping. He zigzagged wildly to avoid men along the path. One managed to stick out a foot and trip him, but Fargo's honed reflexes saved him—for several seconds his arms windmilled the air as he teetered on the feather edge of losing his balance; then he recovered and put on a new burst of speed.

By now a confused alarm rippled through the camp, Mormon guards and others demanding to know what was happening. Enough men had spotted him to give a lively chase, and Fargo realized: He'd never have time to recover his Henry and hop his horse if he didn't force these riled-up men to cover down.

He whirled in midstep and, running backwards, brought the business end of the Spencer up. Aiming high, he levered and fired all seven .56 caliber slugs, spreading them out fanwise. The sounds of pursuit abated long enough for Fargo to grab the Henry, unloop the reins, and vault into the saddle. But then his short grace period was over. Even as he jerked rein and wheeled the black into the street, a fusillade of bullets hurled at him from the camp. The greenhorns, in their zeal to kill, stupidly shot several of their own horses.

Fargo skipped the road and broke out across the open desert, realizing his plan had turned into disaster. True, he could now tell Salt Lake law officers where to find the Landry gang. But by the time he could safely sneak back into town and leave word it would be too late—with Perry dead, Butch and Orrin would have to dust their hocks to a new location.

And what about Old Billy, Fargo wondered. Did he manage to save his own bacon when the shooting commenced?

"Dammitall to hell anyway," Fargo muttered to the black velvet folds of darkness surrounding him. "Can't ride my horse, can't show my Henry, can't even wear my own clothes or beard—there's a reckoning coming, and it better be damn soon."

The only witness who could say for certain exactly what had happened in the outlander camp still lay sprawled on his face where Fargo had buffaloed him, unconscious. Butch Landry and Orrin Trapp quickly realized that no one was paying any attention to them, having rushed to the opposite end of camp to capture the man who had escaped.

"You think it was Fargo?" Trapp asked his boss, keeping his furtive, larval face averted from the mutilated corpse of Harlan Perry.

Butch was rapidly pacing in front of the dying fire, eyes smoky with rage. "I dunno. It ain't Fargo's way to kill a man from ambush. And hell-fire, man, just glom Harlan's skull—it's half gone. I never knowed of Fargo to carry artillery capable of doing that."

"Me neither," Orrin said. "But Deets has forced him to disguise himself, and might be he ain't using his Henry. Whatever done for Harlan sounded like a Big Fifty or an old Hawken gun."

"Never mind all that now," Landry said impatiently, his bull neck again craning around to look at the slumped corpse of their partner. "If it was Fargo, his plan is to get us rail-roaded to the gallows—he knows there's dodgers on us all over the West. Mormon law dogs will soon be crawling like lice all over this camp. It's time to cut loose from these here diggings."

"What about Harlan?"

"What about him? He'll soon be cold as a wagon wheel."

"Ain't we gonna at least bury him?"

Butch swore impatiently. "Orrin, you ain't got the brains God gave a piss-ant! *Bury* him? Where, for crissakes? This ain't the high lonesome where you just plant a man where he drops. 'Sides, them Mormon badge-toters had to hear that shootout—they'll be here quicker than an Indian going to crap."

Both men began to hurriedly collect their saddles and gear.

"It ain't just Mormon law," Butch added. "It's Fargo law, too, and that's the one we got to worry about most. Don't you savvy that? Orrin, if this was Fargo that tossed lead at us tonight *that means he's figured out our plan.* Worse, that top-drawer tracker has *found* us. Mister, our bacon is in the fire. We have to go parlay with Deets—*now*. All three of us are going over the range like Harlan unless we can somehow cut Fargo off at the legs."

17

Fargo expected some hell-bent-for-leather pursuers to give chase as he escaped from the camp, and sure enough he soon heard hooves pounding behind him. He rated Mica's coal black at an open gallop, and while the steed was no Ovaro it stretched itself out with admirable stamina.

Fargo doubted that any of the reckless nickel-chasers behind him could read sign in the darkness, a daunting task even for a veteran frontiersman. Orienting to the polestar, he swung north and ate up the landscape for several miles, then used the cover of a low ridge to swing southwest. When he was satisfied that his pursuers had continued due north, he walked the lathered black for a half mile or so to cool him out. Then he hit leather and, orienting to the Dog Star this time, headed at a canter toward the desert shack.

At first he thought he had missed it in the cloud-draped moonlight. Then the sky overhead cleared in a strong gust and Fargo spotted the tatterdemalion structure. Relief washed over him when he spotted Old Billy's blood bay tethered out back, stripped down to the neck leather.

"Hallo, the shack!" he called out, knowing Old Billy was no man to sneak up on. "Fargo riding in!"

"Ride a cat's tail, you reckless pup! I had you figured for a dead'un by now!"

Fargo lit down, tethered the gelding, and stripped off his saddle and bridle. The horse was still dry, thanks to the easier pace and desert air, so he only watered it from his hat. Old Billy came outside cradling his Greener.

"Fargo, I oughter knock you into next Sunday!"

"Why?" Fargo said innocently, knowing a blast was coming.

"Why?" Billy sputtered. "You must be the joker in this

deck. Prac'ly the minute I slipped into that camp, I spotted all three of them lily-livered mange pots. Trouble was, I couldn't get close enough to get the number of their camp. I was creepin' in slowlike, dang close to reading it, when you blew a tunnel through that big lummox's head. I thought you said no wet work tonight."

"You're the lummox," Fargo replied after drinking warm water from his canteen. "Can't you tell a buffalo gun from an army carbine?"

Old Billy stood silent in the ivory moonlight, letting this point sink in. "Why, that's so, ain't it? My carbine makes a sharp cracking noise. This gun was a boomer."

"Big Fifty," Fargo said, explaining about the man he had buffaloed.

"Well, we carried out our big plan," Old Billy carped. "And for what? For mince pie, that's what. You always say a man wants the element of surprise in a fight, eh? And we lost it tonight. Now them three lubbers know we're on to 'em."

"Two," Fargo replied, "unless you're counting their hired jobber who looks like me."

"Why the hell not count him? Him and the other two are feeding at the same trough, ain't they?"

"Sure, but the element of surprise doesn't count with him—he knows damn well we're after him since that first shooting affray at Mormon Station. As for the other two—I been thinking on it. This botched job tonight might be just the tonic for what ails us."

Old Billy farted with his lips. "Trailsman, I won't swallow your bunk like some will. You're just taking shit and trying to turn it into strawberries."

Fargo shook his head. "You are the most contrary man I know. Think about it. Landry and Trapp dare not stay in that camp—in fact, they're long gone. The Mormon constabulary does not abide gunplay—I'd wager they had that camp cordoned off fifteen minutes after the fracas. Landry and Trapp are owlhoots—they can't afford to be questioned by the law."

"That rings right, but so what? Now we don't know where they are."

"Yeah, but now they have to hole up somewhere or ride

out of this area. Either way, we stand a good chance of crossing their trail. And since the dirt worker's job is done—"

"Done?" Old Billy cut in. "How you figure that? He didn't sink his blade into that Mormon gal—not to mention his pecker."

"Billy, were you mule-kicked in the head as a child? An outlander attacked a Mormon woman and tried to rape and maybe kill her. The fact that he was chased off doesn't amount to a hill of beans. The outrage against Skye Fargo is at a fever pitch and will stay that way until Fargo is captured."

"All right, done and done," Old Billy went along. "I'd chuck all of it for a hot biscuit. Happens you wander near a point, feel free to make it."

Fargo paused to listen to the night, making sure no riders were approaching.

"You know me," he continued. "Given my druthers, I like to play things like the cat who sits near the gopher hole and bides his time. But sometimes you have to bend with the breeze or you break. If we try to wait any longer we'll just be sticking our heads into a noose. So we hunt down all three of these sons of bitches right damn quick."

"Fight or show yellow, huh?"

Billy rubbed his jaw, thinking. "Hell, that's what this hoss favored all along. You was the one argued agin dousing their lights—said we'd kill the proof."

"Oh, I still believe that," Fargo assured him. "Once they're jugged, they'll turn on each other to try and save their own necks. C'mon, let's grab a few hours shut-eye. Then we're going to see if we can cut sign on Landry and Trapp."

"Ain't you forgetting something?" Old Billy said. "Just tonight we was questioned by a Mormon roundsman. We give him the names Neal Bryce and Del Baptiste, said you was a coz to that soldier boy, what's-his-name. Then a war breaks out in the camp. You think the Mormons are too stupid to visit that soldier's wife and ask was we by to say howdy? Hell, she won't even recognize the names."

"So what?" Fargo said as he unbuckled his gun belt. "Did you plan on living forever?"

With dawn still several hours away, Fargo and Old Billy rigged their mounts and headed back across the desert toward Salt Lake City. Desert nights were chilly and they could see their breath forming wraiths of vapor in the silver moonlight. The sky had cleared, showing an explosion of diamond-bright stars and revealing the bleak landscape in a hazy, bluish tint. Stark mountains cut dark silhouettes in the far distance.

"Fargo," Old Billy said, picking up a conversational thread from earlier, "I'm afraid your wick is flickering. After that catawampus you caused in town last night, guards will be swarming that camp like fleas on a hound. And the campers will likely have their own guard set up. We can't just waltz in there, bold as a fat man's ass, and commence to reading sign."

"We don't have to actually enter the town," Fargo replied.

"Then how the hell do we cut sign on them two owl-hoots?"

"Billy, you are a huckleberry above a persimmon when it comes to fretting. Didn't you just say, a few days ago, that I'm good at thinking like a criminal?"

Old Billy snorted. "Aye, but you needn't sound proud of it."

"Well, here's some criminal thinking: Landry and Trapp had to dust their hocks out of there damn quick, right? It don't seem likely they had a fallback position in Salt Lake City—not being gentiles and wanted men. That means they had to bust out across the desert."

"That rings right so far. But, Fargo, you of all hombres know how hard it is to pick up a trail even when you got an idea where to look. Crissakes, them two mighta pulled foot from anyplace."

"That won't spend," Fargo gainsaid. "Unless they haven't got more brains than a rabbit, they sure as hell didn't ride north through the middle of the city. And they wouldn't head west—I headed that way with a passel of armed heel-flies after me. That means they most likely went east or south."

"Uh-huh. And east would take them right back to Echo Canyon where they was. A good hidey-hole for criminals—no law."

"Yeah, but could their Fargo impersonator go back there?"

Old Billy mulled that. "'Course not. He'd avoid it like the mouth of hell. He was Doc Jacoby when he was there. And Jacoby lit out right after that Louise what's-her-name pulled her own plug—or so he said."

"Now you're whistling. And I'm after believing that wherever Landry and Trapp go, the dirt worker will have to be there too. That leaves due south. You know this territory—what's located halfway between Salt Lake City and Utah Lake?"

"Why, Bingham Canyon. It's just a whoop and a holler from here."

"The way you say," Fargo agreed. "We'll find the most likely beeline between town and the canyon and look for tracks."

"That's casting a mighty wide net," Old Billy said, "when a feller's lookin' for something as small as horseshoe tracks in the Salt Desert. But you're a top hand in that line, Fargo, and leastways it'll keep us out of the city."

A grin eased Fargo's lips apart. "Well, after we scour for prints we *will* be heading back into the city."

Old Billy suddenly reined in. Fargo tugged rein and met his partner's eyes, the grin spreading into a smile.

"Fargo, don't blow smoke up my ass! Happens we set foot among that Mormon tribe, they'll baste our bacon! The hell you got planned?"

"You do want your horse back, don't you?" Fargo demanded.

"Not just this minute! You yourself said these horses of Mica's is good animals."

"Sure, they're good stable horses, like all of Mica's. But we're headed across the Great Salt, and these mounts have been stall-fed too long. The army is out there looking for our dust, Old Billy, and I'd rather have my Ovaro under me. And your Appaloosa is damn near as reliable."

"Horse apples! I'm dead-set against it," Old Billy insisted. "The plan was to hide our horses until we gut-hook this gang. Happens we ride into that town now, after the ruckus in the camp, we're both gone beavers."

"Stretching the blanket a mite, ain't you?" Fargo said as he gigged his horse forward again. "We're making the final push now, and we need the best horses—not just good ones. Of course, if the great Indian fighter can't pull his own freight, I s'pose I can go it alone."

"Fargo, you mouthy pup, I can not only cut the bacon, I can dish you up a heap of crow! It makes me ireful, is all."

"Then get over your peeve," Fargo shot back. "We've spent enough damn time waiting for our enemy's attack. Now it's time to take the bull by the horns and throw the son of a bitch."

Another hour of moonlight riding brought them within sight of the campground, where a few fires still blazed— sentry posts, Fargo guessed. The two riders found a slight draw and dismounted, hobbling their mounts.

"If Landry and Trapp sneaked out of camp," Fargo mused aloud, "they'd want to get onto the desert as quick as they could. That means they would've crossed somewhere right around here."

"Why'n't we just take it for a fact that they done it?" Old Billy asked. "Then we just pound our saddles to Bingham Canyon."

"That idea's not half bad," Fargo admitted as he went down on all fours. "Trouble is, we waste too much time if we're wrong. Besides, the Mormon army is out there somewhere, and they're experts at relay riding when they're on to a quarry. I don't mind rolling the dice, but there better be money in the hat."

Fargo began a slow crawl straight to the east, hoping to cross a due-south trail. Moonlight was generous, and he had kept his hat pulled down over his eyes for the past half hour, adjusting his vision for total darkness. Now the desert floor was as visible as if in early daylight.

"Wind's been still tonight," he remarked to Old Billy. "I see a fox trail that's not filled in yet. Looks to be just a few hours old."

Another half hour passed without luck, and Old Billy cast an exasperated sigh. "Hell, Fargo, we're just washing bricks. Looks like maybe they pointed their bridles toward Echo Canyon."

"And it looks like you're full of sheep dip," Fargo announced triumphantly. "Glom these."

Kneecaps cracking loudly, Old Billy squatted beside his partner. Making sure their bodies blocked it from the camp, Fargo struck a lucifer to life with his thumbnail.

"Why, they're clear as blood spoor in new snow," Old Billy admitted. "You can see it's a gallop by the way they overlap. But—there's three horses."

"Only two carry riders. The third is on a lead-line behind the horse on the left. Harlan Perry's mount. They left the body—big surprise, huh?"

Old Billy looked straight ahead across the desert floor. "You called their play, Trailsman. Ain't nothing out there until you get to Bingham Canyon."

"*We'll* be out there just as soon as we switch out these horses for our own," Fargo reminded him. "But we best hurry, old son. I see false dawn in the east, and the real thing won't be far behind."

18

They returned to the two rented horses and Fargo began to loosen his saddle.

"The hell you up to, Fargo?" Old Billy demanded. "This ain't no time for the currycomb."

"Sometimes," Fargo replied, "even a blind hog will root up an acorn."

"That blind hog would be me?"

Fargo nodded. "You were right, Old Billy. We can't expect to ride into Salt Lake City *and* back out. We've both got fast horses and we can bust out, with luck. But we're going to sneak to Mica's livery on foot. Strip that bay."

Old Billy followed orders. "But, say, what about these here horses?"

"We leave 'em tethered right here and tell Mica where they are. Hell, they're in no danger except from wolf packs, and wolves hole up around this time."

"That shines," Billy agreed. "Mica's got his brand on their hips—a man would have to be a puddin' brain to steal a branded horse in Mormon country."

Both men heaved their rigs over a shoulder and headed toward the city.

"Mica's livery is on the western outskirts," Fargo said, thinking out loud. "So we swing wide of the camps and stay behind the buildings. With luck we can give the slip to the guards—it's the damn dogs we need to watch."

The sky lightened as the two men trudged into town, selecting a narrow alley that ran between wooden warehouses.

Old Billy paused to peer through a window of one of the buildings.

"The hell you up to?" Fargo called back over his shoulder.

"I wunner if there's any cheerwater inside. I'm dry as a year-old cow chip."

"This is Salt Lake City, you muttonhead, not San Francisco."

Old Billy's tongue brushed his wind-cracked lips. "Well, where do we get a bottle?"

Fargo waved this off and hurried forward. "You're building a pimple into a peak. Plenty of time later to worry about a bottle."

"Huh! Easy to say for them as ain't got the tormentin' thirst on 'em."

Fargo wasn't even listening now—he had reached the end of the alley and spotted Mica's livery across the wide, wagon-rutted street.

He saw no guards or any other signs of life, just a wagon yard and a feed store beyond the livery barn. Just as he stepped into the street, however, a pack of yellow curs emerged from behind the feed store.

Fargo froze in place, knowing movement would catch their eyes more than shape. He knew it was the dogs' incredible sense of smell that was his worst enemy, and fortunately he stood in a crosswind—a wind, however, that could shift at any moment. He raised a hand behind him to halt Old Billy.

The curs, following their leader, padded down the middle of the street in the ghostly half-light. Fargo knew they'd spot him if they didn't smell him first. He was still considering how to play this when Old Billy edged his white-streaked head around the corner of the building just enough to see the danger.

His hand moved to his sash and removed the bolos. In a trice he cocked back his right arm, gave a hard, rotating toss. Fargo watched the round, leather-wrapped stones twirl at blurring speed into the midst of the pack. Billy had no intention of bringing down any of the dogs—only of scattering them, and scatter like ninepins they did. The bolos skimmed along the ground, frightening them and parting them like the Red Sea. The pack subdivided into two and raced off without even a whimper.

"Good work, old campaigner," Fargo praised. "You're a good man to take along."

Old Bill retrieved his bolos, and the two men slipped into Mica's livery.

"Be you friend or foe?" a rasping voice demanded from halfway down the stalls. "A load of double aught is pointed right atcha."

"Lower your hammers, Mica," Fargo called back. "It's just me and Old Billy. We're here to fetch our mounts."

"I heerd that ruckus last night, Trailsman. How many fresh souls did you send to heaven?"

"Truth to tell," Fargo replied, "I didn't send any nor did Old Billy. One owlhoot did get in the way of a bullet, though, and it's good odds he took the south fork into hell."

Mica, pulling up his gallowses, emerged from the stall where he'd been sleeping. "Where's my horses? Kilt?"

"Naw, they're fine." Fargo explained where they'd been left and why. "You'll be paid for the extra trouble, old-timer."

"You'll find a bag of oats outside the Ovaro's stall. Both your hosses has been fed up good."

Fargo and Old Billy quickly tacked their horses in the meager light. Mica spread a piece of cheesecloth on a workbench. "Likely you two sons of trouble are low on eats, and sure as glory you can't stock up around these diggin's."

The two men interrupted their labors to watch him pack the cloth with beans, hardtack, and dried fruit.

"Mica, we're beholden," Fargo said.

"Damn my eyes," Old Billy said, staring at the food. "I wouldn't mind getting outside of some grub right now. I'm so hungry my backbone is scraping against my ribs."

"Push that thought from your mind," Fargo told him as he slipped the bit into the Ovaro's mouth. "We'll grab some chuck when we're well shed of this town."

"How 'bout that jug of yours, Mica?" Old Billy said. "Mind if I take a sup of mash?"

"Huh! Now you want somethin' from me you're polite as pie. Help yourself—it's in that tool cubby beside the harness board."

"Gradual on that," Fargo snapped when Old Billy set the

jug on his shoulder and took several deep, sweeping slugs. "I want you sober when we bust out of town. Lead *will* fly."

"Damn straight it will," Old Billy retorted when he saw that Fargo was changing into his buckskins. "I reckon you *want* to get us killed?"

Fargo felt his chin. "Here's how I figure it. My beard is starting to come back in, and I'm riding the Ovaro again. So why not quit cowering behind summer names and be Fargo again? I want my toothpick back in my boot and my Henry in the scabbard, too. Let these plug-ugly sons of bucks know just who's sending them across the River Jordan."

"By God!" Old Billy approved. "It made sense at first to disguise yourself, but hell, you done milked that grift."

"Skye Fargo rides agin," Old Mica chimed in. "It gives me the fantods, Trailsman, to see you wearing reach-me-downs. Buckskins is your natch'ral gait."

Fargo felt the soft hide against his skin and had to agree. He accepted the food from Mica and stuffed it into a saddle pocket. Then he stuck his head out the livery door and looked carefully all around just as the sun broke over the eastern flats.

"All clear right now," he told Old Billy. "We're going out the same way we sneaked in—through alleys and between buildings. If it stays quiet we'll go slow. If we ride into a shit storm we'll pound our horses. If somebody tosses lead at us, don't bother to fire back—killing a Mormon won't win us any jewels in paradise."

Fargo led the Ovaro out into the paddock. Before he forked leather he pressed a gold eagle into Mica's gnarled hand.

"H'ar now!" the old salt protested. "You don't owe me no ten dollars, Fargo."

Old Billy stared with covetous eyes at the gold coin. "Christ Jesus, Fargo! He's right."

"Both you jays pipe down," Fargo said. "Billy, keep your eyes to all sides. As the story goes, there was a young Mormon woman attacked by Skye Fargo. And woe betide any shit-heel trail tramp siding him."

Fargo could feel his stallion quivering with the desire to run full throttle in the early morning chill. He kept shortening the reins to control the Ovaro's head. The two mounts walked slowly and quietly through a maze of alleys. Twice the men reined in as they reached wide, creosote-oiled streets. After a careful check they gigged their horses quickly across the streets.

By now the dull red orb of the sun was well above the horizon, and the streets of Salt Lake City were beginning to fill and thicken. One more street lay ahead, and Fargo heaved a sigh of relief. That sigh, however, quickly snagged in the back of his throat when they reached the street and glanced right. He spotted a line of huge, lumbering wagons with high wheels and long double-teams of mules.

"Freight caravan," he told Old Billy. "Ten, twelve wagons. We'll have to fade back into the alley until they pass."

He pulled straight back on the reins and the well-trained Ovaro pranced backward into the obscuring shadows between two rows of homes.

"This'll take a while," Fargo fretted, listening to the bullwhackers snapping their long blacksnake whips and cursing like stable sergeants. "By the time we get across we're bound to be spotted. Well, leastways we'll be out in the open and we can give our mounts their head."

Old Billy said nothing. Curious, Fargo gave him an over-the-shoulder glance and found the Indian fighter staring intently through a window on a level with his face.

"The hell are you doing?" Fargo demanded. But Old Billy clearly didn't even hear him. Eyes unblinking, his breathing hoarse and quick, he continued to stare through the window.

Fargo wheeled the Ovaro around and rode up beside his mesmerized partner. "Get away from that window," he ordered sternly. "You want somebody to spot you and raise the hue and cry?"

"Fargo," Old Billy croaked hoarsely, "stand off or I'll shoot you. Never come between a dog and his meat."

Fargo glanced inside and felt his heart give a jump. Two young women, obviously twin sisters, lay on their backs asleep in a big brass bed. Evidently they had pulled off their nightclothes to take advantage of the cooler temperature. Blood throbbing in his ears and palms, Fargo took in their long russet hair, full, sensuous lips, and smooth marble skin.

Their breasts—as identical as their faces—were full, heavy, and pendant with nipples the color of fruit wine.

The deltas of hair between their legs were dark and mysterious, inviting a man's imagination to think about the warm dampness tucked just behind those silken portals. Fargo did think about it, and almost simultaneously both men were forced to adjust themselves in the saddle. Fargo thought about his recent conquests in Echo Canyon and at Kellar's Station. Both women were delightful, but he had not supped full enough.

"Good . . . god . . . *damn*," Old Billy muttered hoarsely. "Whoever said you can't tell a Mormon's women from his oxen is full of shit up to his ears. Fargo, you've screwed prac'ly every woman on the continent and much of their livestock. How's them two rate?"

"Blue ribbons," Fargo replied, tearing his eyes away reluctantly. "Now move clear, Old Billy. The charge against me in these parts is raping, cutting, and killing women. How will things stand if we get caught ogling these two?"

Old Billy nodded, enjoying one last look. "That rings right. 'Sides, it ain't much pleasure staring at women that comely and knowing I can't bull 'em. It's like staring at another man's money knowing I'll never spend it."

The men nudged their mounts a few feet away. Old Billy shivered. "I gotta haul my freight to a whore first chance I get. I'll think on them two dumplings and then ride that soiled dove until she smokes and throws off sparks. I never seen—"

The sudden, loud thump of a window sash being thrown open interrupted Old Billy. Fargo slewed quickly around in his saddle and felt his face drain cold: A stout Mormon matron in a flannel nightgown and nightcap aimed a scattergun at the two men in the alley.

"I'll teach you heathen outlanders to rape *my* daughters!" she said in a homicidal voice as her finger wrapped the trigger.

Fargo did some quick horseback thinking. They were mere eyeblinks away from disaster, and even the Ovaro couldn't get ahead of buckshot. Nor could he and Old Billy pull down on the woman in time. Even if they could, she was too angry to be deterred, and they could hardly shoot her—they had, after all, been peeping at her girls through the window.

There was only one option, and weak though it was, Fargo chose it.

"Left fender!" he barked at Old Billy. "Pull foot!"

Old Billy had been in enough close-in scrapes to instantly understand. Both men, borrowing a trick from Plains Indian warriors, slumped down the left side of their saddles, putting their horses between the most vital parts of their anatomy and the outraged woman with the scattergun. Simultaneously, they thumped their mounts into motion.

But even as their horses leaped, both barrels of the scattergun exploded behind them. A stinging fire raced up the arm Fargo was holding the saddle horn with as well as the exposed right leg he could not jerk from the stirrup in time. The Ovaro, too, had taken some of the load and shot into the wide street heedless of the freight caravan.

Despite the pain like a hundred snakebites, Fargo silently rejoiced—he had been hind-ended enough to recognize rock salt when he felt it, a painful but nonlethal load. However, the outraged woman wasn't done with these gentile criminals yet.

"Skye Fargo!" she screeched out the open window. "It's Skye Fargo! Him and that purple-faced monkey tried to outrage my girls! Help!"

The teamsters and bullwhackers were outlanders and in no hurry to take up any Mormon cause. They gaped, slack-jawed with astonishment, as the two riders streaked across the street, causing several startled mules to rear in the traces. But enough armed Mormons were in the street and heard the woman's cry.

Rifles and handguns cracked behind them as the fleeing pair broke onto the white-salt desert flat, rating their horses at a full run. Plumes of sand kicked up around them as bullets sought their vitals.

"Fargo!" Billy roared from just behind him. "My ass feels like it's been panther-chewed! Damn you to hell anyway!"

"*You're* the jackass who stared through the window first,"

Fargo replied without turning around. "But it's too dead to skin now. We got another problem: Won't be long and there'll be a posse dogging us all the way to Bingham Canyon. It's still cool now, so push that Appaloosa hard, old son. Unless we open out a big lead now, we'll be picking lead out of our livers."

19

Captain Saunders Lee called for a ten-minute rest. He lit down from his big, dust-coated cavalry sorrel and held the reins as he surveyed the bleak terrain surrounding the Mormon soldiers. The men had lost their bearings in the last dust storm and he searched for any landmark that might help to orient them.

The brutal afternoon sun coaxed out a thick layer of sweat that mixed with the dust coating his skin, forming an irritating paste under the collar of his tunic. He was filthy, hungry, thirsty, and worn down to the nub—even the wet heat of tropical Mexico had not been as torturous as this bone-dry desert air that evaporated a man's piss before it hit the ground.

The burly form of Sergeant Shoemaker trudged up beside him. "Are we lost, sir, or just 'momentarily bewildered'?"

Saunders managed a slight grin at that one. "That's enough guff from you, Sergeant. Follow my finger."

He pointed east. The wind-driven grit made it difficult to open their eyes beyond mere slits.

"See how there seems to be a sheen of light out on the horizon?"

"Yessir. Glows like an angel's halo."

"That has to be Utah Lake. It's fresh water and fresh water reflects more than salt water."

Shoemaker nodded. "But Utah Lake sits right on the west flank of the Wasatch. Why can't we see the mountains?"

"We will in an hour or so. But right now there's an optical ruse going on. That's all pure white sand over there with lots of quartz and mica in it. The sun is at a perfect angle to reflect it like a shield—the water glare can be seen but not the solid mountains."

"Well, sir, so *that's* why officers go to college. Optical ruse, huh?"

"College?" Saunders shot back. "I'd give four years at West Point to sleep on a shuck mattress tonight."

"The men share your sentiments. Right now they're keen to turn Skye Fargo's guts into tepee ropes. You think he's still around here?"

"Maybe, but it's a damn long chance. Unless he foxed us and stayed in the city somehow. Fargo is the type to head toward the trouble, not away from it. All he can accomplish out here is drying himself to jerky."

"Well then, Corporal Hudson is poorly, sir. Centipede got into his boot. Was you to declare a medical emergency we'd have to get him back to headquarters on the double."

Saunders considered this. A centipede sting was hardly fatal, under normal circumstances, but could indeed kill a man in these grueling conditions. Besides, they'd been patrolling the desert for days with no sign of anyone but a few Indians.

"Let me make one last reconnoiter with the glasses," he finally decided, unbuckling a saddle pocket and removing his binoculars. "Then we'll head back."

"*That's* the gait, sir. You've got me half convinced that Fargo is innocent, so who wants to slap him in irons?"

Saunders raised his glasses and focused them out past the middle distance. He swept the empty, flat desert to the west, then north toward Great Salt Lake. He aimed them east toward Salt Lake City and then scanned slowly south toward the outlying settlement of Murray and, finally, Bingham Canyon.

"We've struck a lode," he said abruptly.

Shoemaker tensed like a hound on point. "Fargo, sir?"

"It's two men riding at breakneck speed. One's wearing buckskins and riding a pinto stallion. The other man is astride a golden Appaloosa."

"Sounds like Fargo and his chum, all right. If so, he's back in his own clothes and riding his own horse."

Saunders watched a little while longer, adjusting the focus. "Oh, I'd bet a dollar to a doughnut it's Fargo and Old Billy, all right. About two miles behind them there's a town posse."

Shoemaker said, "Where they headed?"

"Has to be Bingham Canyon. It's all hard mountains after

that—mountains bristling with warpath Utes. Fargo knows that canyon well—ten years ago he scouted and mapped it for the City Council."

Saunders' entire mien changed as he shook off his weariness and looked suddenly alert. "Sergeant," he said, lowering the glasses, "tell the men to prepare for contact phase. Quickly water the horses and make sure weapons are operating. Then mount up. But remember—*no* weapon is to be fired unless we're fired upon. I want these men taken alive."

"See anything?" Orrin Trapp asked in a voice tight with nervousness.

"Not a damn thing," Butch Landry replied. "But it's dusty as all git-out. If that cussed wind dies down we'll be able to see better."

Deets Gramlich, working his teeth with a hog-bristle toothbrush, stood behind both men. He pulled it from his mouth and said, "He's coming, all right. Fargo isn't called the Trailsman for nothing. Wind or no wind, dust or no dust, he'll spot your trail and know where you headed."

"Why put it on us?" Landry snarled. "Unless you miracled your ass here you musta left a trail."

"I doubled around and came in from the West Mountains District. This was supposed to be our emergency fallback position, remember? Why didn't the two of you just leave a trail of bread crumbs?"

"We told you how Fargo *found* us and had already killed Harlan," Trapp replied in a low voice laced with menace. "We had no time for fancy parlor tricks."

The three men were ensconced in the hollow of a basalt turret known as the Crow's Nest—a rock spire on the right-hand side of the only entrance into Bingham Canyon. A series of trap-rock shelves formed a crude stairway up to the hollow. A squat edifice of mud and lumber, with its hind end backed into the side of the turret, had been built within the hollow years earlier for a sniper position against Indians. From here the three men could, weather permitting, see for miles across the glaring desert and command a clear shot at anyone riding into the canyon. The shadowed stone of the canyon walls surrounded them like black curtains.

"This ain't what I wanted," Landry spat out bitterly. "He was never s'posed to know about me, Harlan, and Orrin being in the mix. Deets was s'posed to get him jugged and then hanged. Now it's all come a cropper and all three of us is holding the crappy end of the stick."

"It's coming down to a goddamn shootout," Orrin chimed in. "A shootout with two men who can knock out the eyes of a pheasant at two hundred yards."

Deets tossed back his head and laughed. He no longer wore any Fargo disguise, but still bore a striking resemblance to the Trailsman.

"Boys, you need to reach down inside your pants and see if you own a set! Fargo is indeed a formidable enemy, but don't go puny and confuse the man with the myth. He bleeds red like all the rest of us."

Landry craned his neck around to look at the actor. "You wanna chew that a little finer?"

"You can still triumph. It *hasn't* come a cropper. Fargo is still a fugitive, and even if he has linked me to you, he can hardly go to law about it."

Landry mulled that. "All right, I like the tune. Keep singing."

"First we kill Old Billy—we have to concentrate on Fargo, but we can't until Billy Williams is out of the mix. That bastard is dangerous as a she-grizz with cubs. Then we *wound* Skye Fargo—wound him bad enough to take the fight out of him. I'm a good trail doctor and I can stem any bleeding. Then you two let me use my skills to alter your appearance a little so you can go back to Salt Lake City. I'll take Fargo in after dying my hair and gluing on a mustache. If we play it right, Fargo will never have to see any of us the way we really look."

Deets had no intention of carrying out this plan—he had a far better one in mind, and Fargo would indeed have to die for it to succeed. But Old Billy was truly a threat and required killing. And Deets had no illusions about killing Fargo unless he was wounded first—preferably by one of these two fools.

Landry and Trapp exchanged a long glance after the suggestion.

"It *could* work," Trapp suggested. "Me, I'd favor a simpler plan. But we got nothing better."

Landry slowly nodded his bulldog head. "Too rich for my belly—too many 'ifs' and 'ands.' Still, I reckon it's better than a poke in the eye with a sharp stick."

"*Now* you're whistling!" Deets exclaimed. "I get the rest of my gold shiners, you fellows get your revenge, and Skye Fargo does the hurt dance—on air."

Twisting around in the saddle without slowing the Ovaro's pace, Fargo broke out his spyglasses and studied the glaring white expanse of desert behind them.

"A couple of their horses are foundering," he announced. "I knew those town nags wouldn't keep pace once the heat rose. We've got a good lead on them."

"That's just hunky-dory," Old Billy barbed, "but my horse is lathered and your Ovaro is blowing foam, too."

Fargo nodded, hauling back on the reins. "Let's lead 'em for a spell to cool 'em out. We'll want these mounts rested when we rush that canyon."

Old Billy, too, pulled up and lit down, leading his Appaloosa by the bridle reins. "Rush the canyon?"

"Did I stutter? We'll have to, old son, because of the Crow's Nest. It's a fortified sniper's nest above the entrance. They'll have a straight bead on us when we approach across the open desert."

"Can these bald-face baboons shoot?"

"Whoever cut loose on us at the bathing pool near Mormon Station seemed like a fair hand with the Henry—assuming he's in the canyon. As for Butch Landry and Orrin Trapp, I'd rate each fair-to-middling. They made things lively for me in the Big Bend country. We'll have to hit that canyon at a two twenty clip, zigzagging to throw off their bead, and come in a-smokin' to keep them covered down."

Old Billy again failed to muster any spit and unleashed a string of curses that would make a horse blush. "Why, Christ! So we make it into the canyon without being shot to ribbons. What then? Them three got the high ground. And then we got this clusterfuck from Salt Lake City on our ampersands—if they don't kill their horses first, they'll be dealing us misery."

Fargo trudged through the hot sand, eyes closed to slits against the glare. "What then, huh? We climb the staircase ledges and smoke those rats out of their hole, that's what. That Greener of yours should put the fear of God into 'em. And we hope like hell that my twin is up there, too, and that we get some evidence for the posse. Otherwise . . ."

"Otherwise," Old Billy took over, "we get caught with nothing but our dicks in our hands. That posse might be nothing but ignunt townies, but there's a smart chance of guns among 'em—more than we can cut down."

"The way you say," Fargo agreed, glancing west and trying to see through the glaring haze. He pulled out his binoculars again and studied the terrain. "Pile on the agony," he finally muttered.

"Utes?" Old Billy demanded. "You want I should break out Sir Richard?"

"Won't work with this bunch. No Utes—looks like Mormon cavalry headed straight for the canyon. They musta spotted us."

"I'll be go to hell," Old Billy lamented. "We're caught in a pincers trap. It's the calaboose for sure unless the lead colic kills us."

Fargo looked over at him, strong white teeth flashing through his new beard stubble. "The hell? Old Billy, if you looked any lower you'd be walking on your lip. This is what you live for. Why, I might even get you killed."

The dust-powdered Indian fighter perked up considerably. "Square deal! Blood, guts, the disgustin' sound of a sucking chest wound. Hell's bells, mebbe I'll get *you* killed, Trailsman! No thorn without a rose, eh?"

20

"Two riders," Deets finally announced in the tone of a preacher predicting salvation. He closed his telescope. "I can't make them out in this dust, but you know who it has to be."

Landry worked the lever of his Volcanic repeating rifle, jacking a round into the chamber. "We'll have clear beads when they get closer. Remember the plan: We kill Old Billy first, then shoot to wound Fargo."

Deets checked the loads in the Henry's tube magazine and knelt between the two men, laying the Henry's barrel across the low wall of the sniper's nest.

"You ever shot a man, Deets?" Orrin asked as he laid his ammo pouch atop the wall. "I mean one that's tossing lead back, not sneak killings like you done back near Echo Canyon. It ain't nothing like using a sticker the way you done on that actress."

Landry shot Orrin a warning glance, and all of an instant Deets realized which way the wind set. So the gang had known all along that he was wanted for murder under his real name—just as they likely knew he was carrying with him all the gold they'd paid him so far. A man wanted for murder might horse-trade with the law to save his neck. Deets knew, thanks to that one careless remark, that he was marked for death.

And one thing he had learned from Skye Fargo himself was to always claim the first waltz.

"The actress?" he replied casually, propping his Henry against the wall and pretending to reach for his canteen. "That was what they term a crime of passion. The man who kills in cold blood is the boy you want to give the slip to."

In a snake-swift movement his right hand wrapped the butt of his Colt and shucked it out of the holster, thumb-cocking it at the same time. At almost point-blank range he squeezed the trigger, blowing a spray of bloody brain curdles out the side of Butch Landry's head. With perfect choreography he cocked and fired at Orrin Trapp before he could even react.

"It was coming anyway, gents," he told the pair of slumped corpses. "But I did hope to count on you for the shooting affray."

Nonetheless, Deets knew he commanded a fine position here above the entrance to the canyon. And he had grown quite adept with the Henry. Fortune favored the bold, and he had indeed been bold from the outset.

He searched the dead men's clothing. Orrin carried forty dollars in quarter-eagles, a useful sum, but the chamois pouch inside Landry's shirt yielded five hundred in double-eagles. Deets knew he would find much more in the saddlebags of Landry's dapple gray, tethered below with the rest of the horses in a niche of the canyon's striated rock walls.

Deets turned his attention to the two approaching riders, now visible without spyglasses. The "simple plan" Orrin had wished for was now in play: kill both men. That was a tall order, and once it was done, more work remained. He would have to tie a rope around Fargo's ankles and General Taylor's saddle horn, dragging Fargo swiftly over the sharp rock spines and prickly-pear cactus of the canyon floor.

The resulting damage would destroy much of Fargo's features. He would then don his Fargo disguise and claim that he shot it out with the criminal Fargo look-alike on the staircase ledges and the fake Trailsman fell—and then Deets would be the "real" Fargo, his name cleared, the women and fame all his to enjoy. And not only would he have the Landry gang's gold, he would collect on the reward for them. No one in Utah Territory would be surprised when Skye by-God Fargo rode into Salt Lake City leading three horses with a desperado slumped over each. He would leave General Taylor for the Indians to claim and take possession of Fargo's storied pinto.

Deets glanced at the two bodies, now surrounded by

pools of blood. Then he studied the riders, still closing in at an easy pace. Five more minutes and they'd be in rifle range. He dropped to his knees, as if praying, and laid the Henry's long barrel across the wall.

"One bullet, one enemy," he said softly as he clicked the hammer back.

Fargo and Old Billy had rested their mounts for one last burst of breakneck speed. Both men held their rifles in their right hands, muzzles pointing straight up, butt-plates resting on their thighs. When it was time to fire, they would seize the reins in their teeth to free up both hands.

"We're nudging into range," Fargo said, "and we're riding into the sun, not out of it. Hit that canyon full throttle, old son, and then haul your freight up them ledges with Patsy Plumb on point. That express gun will blow them outta that nest if they don't show the white feather. I'll keep them hunkered down with the Henry."

"I'm keen for a frolic," Old Billy assured him. "But them soldiers is closing on our right flank. Why'n't we just let them tie the ribbon?"

"I like that, but it's possible that citizens' rabble behind us will beat them to the canyon. That bunch of pus-gut hotheads could open up on us. I'd prefer to hand over some prisoners. If it looks like the soldiers will make it first, let's hold off while I make medicine with Saunders Lee."

Old Billy opened his mouth to speak when his slouch hat suddenly spun off his head. A heartbeat later the familiar crack of a Henry reached them.

"Here's the fandango!" Fargo shouted, adding a whoop. "Quarter the wind, Old Billy!"

In a classic cavalry maneuver under fire, each man peeled off to his flank in a sharp ninety-degree turn, then worked the reins sharply to form zigzag riding patterns as they "quartered" back around to the front. Fargo quickly realized only one man was firing—albeit rapidly and accurately—and worried that the other two might be in different locations.

White plumes of desert sand pimpled the ground around the Ovaro's hooves, and bullets snapped past Fargo's ears.

One zipped by so close that he felt the wind rip and heard an angry-hornet sound.

By now he had located the muzzle flash from above and took the reins in his teeth, bringing the Henry down to the ready and opening fire. Old Billy's Spencer joined his Henry as the two men rained lead on the Crow's Nest.

Deets Gramlich was forced to kiss the ground when the two seasoned marksmen below found their range and peppered his position. With his hands shaking it was difficult to reload the Henry's tricky tube magazine. Finally the withering wall of lead abated and he guessed they were reloading too.

He hazarded a peek over the low wall and felt his face go numb: The dust swirls had settled, and from due north came a ragtag but well-armed posse; from due west, galloping in a flying-wedge formation, came a dozen men wearing the smart, light-gray uniforms of the Mormon Battalion. And the towhead soldier leading them must be Captain Saunders Lee—Deets had read about him in the Salt Lake newspaper.

Panic pinched his throat shut. Even if he could kill Fargo, it was too late now. Only his skills as an actor might save him. He glanced at his saddlebag and tossed the Henry aside. There was only one chance, and he would have to hurry. This would be the most important performance of his life, and if it didn't pass muster, he would become the sorriest son of a bitch in seventeen states.

"Hold it," Fargo said, raising one hand to halt Old Billy. "I think our favorite boy has one more rabbit to pull out of his hat. And maybe we best let him pull it."

The two men sat their saddles just inside the narrow entrance to the canyon. Banded rock walls surrounded them.

"The hell?" Old Billy carped. "You're the one said we had to go up them staircase ledges a-smokin'. That posse ain't but a stone's throw behind us now. You was right, Trailsman— we need something to give them before they burn us down."

Fargo's hawk eyes searched the area as he spoke. "The soldiers are going to beat them, and Saunders won't let his men open the ball without permission. Besides, I think there's only one man up in the Crow's Nest, and I'm damned if I'm going to kill him—that would be showing him mercy. C'mon."

Fargo had spotted a declivity in the east wall. Arching his neck to carefully inspect the ledges leading up to the sniper's nest, he led Old Billy to the narrow fissure.

"I'll be clemmed," Billy muttered when they discovered four horses: a dapple gray, a big roan with a blazed forehead, a tan with a black mane and tail, and a black-and-white pinto remarkably similar to the Ovaro. All were still saddled except the tan.

"The one without a saddle must be Harlan Perry's," Fargo speculated. "They skedaddled from Salt Lake City so fast they left it behind."

"That shines, but don't this sorter queer your notion about there being only one hombre up topside? Or do you think mebbe they're holed up someplace else in the canyon?"

Fargo shook his head. "I mapped this place, and there's damn few good places to hole up for a gunfight. I think all three men went up there, all right. But only one was plinking at us. I got a hunch that the man who's left powder-burned the other two for some reason."

Hooves were pounding close now, from north and west, and Fargo hoped the soldiers made it first.

Old Billy rubbed his chin. "And you're thinkin' it was your twin brother what done the killing?"

Fargo inclined his head toward the horses. "Two of them still have their saddlebags. But not the pinto. Our master of disguises has an ace up his sleeve, and I say let's let him play it."

Riders were about to enter the canyon. Fargo swung down, holding the reins in one hand and placing the other high over his head to show it held no weapons. Old Billy followed suit. A swirl of white alkali dust blew into the entrance followed by Captain Saunders Lee on a dust-powdered sorrel. His squad filed in behind him, weapons at the ready.

"Well, your beard's half chewed off," the officer greeted Fargo, "but you *look* like Fargo. I'm afraid you're under arrest, old chum."

"Won't be the first time," Fargo replied calmly. "How 'bout Old Billy here?"

"'Fraid so. Accomplice and accessory."

"You should know the shit I got away with," Old Billy boasted. "Makes these charges look like spider leavings."

"I recommend you wait around here a bit," Fargo said. "Three men rode in before us. You'll find their horses hidden right behind us. One of those horses, by the way, is a dead ringer for my Ovaro."

Saunders perked up at this intelligence. Before he could check on the horses, however, the mob from Salt Lake City arrived, led by a stern-featured Mormon with a wreath beard. He wore the red arm patch of a constable.

"The situation is under control, Justin," Saunders informed him. "We'll bring the prisoners back to the city. First we have to investigate the canyon."

"You investigate all you want. But Fargo and the stain-face heathen with him go back with us. They broke civilian law. Everyone knows you're friends with Fargo, Captain Lee. Why, you haven't even divested them of their weapons."

Old Billy fumed at the insult to him. "Honest, Constable, me and Fargo was only helping that sheep over the fence."

"Bottle it," Fargo snapped. Before the constable could react, however, a voice startled them.

"I see you've caught the imposter. Good work, gentlemen."

As one, all heads swiveled toward the staircase ledges. Jaws went slack at sight of yet another Skye Fargo standing hip-cocked on the bottom ledge. The buckskins, the perfect square-cut beard much fuller than the other Fargo's, the Henry tossed over one shoulder, the walnut-grip Colt, the formidable Arkansas toothpick in a boot sheath—at a glance he seemed more authentic than the Fargo standing below.

"Hallo, Saunders!" he called out. "Been a coon's age, old friend! If I were you, I'd get those two reprobates disarmed immediately."

Saunders glanced back and forth between the two mirror images, his face a mask of confusion.

"Sold!" the constable roared out. "So it was true all along. This scurvy knave with the half-baked beard *was* hiding behind Fargo's identity. I never believed Fargo would kill women."

Fargo laughed. "So you gents believe this pretty picture

off the cover of a half-dimer is the real Fargo, eh? Then why is Old Billy Williams with me?"

"He's not," the replica Fargo chimed in smoothly. "You murdered Old Billy back in Nebraska Territory and almost got me. That's just some shit-heel owlhoot you picked up in Jackson Hole."

"Has anybody here ever met Old Billy?" Saunders called out. An ominous silence greeted his question.

"I'll be et fir a tater," Old Billy muttered. "I'm murdered and didn't even know it."

"If you're the real Fargo," Saunders interceded, looking at the man on the ledge, "when's the last time we saw each other?"

"In Powder River country. We got into a little frolic with some Northern Cheyenne renegades. Lasted three days. We holed up in an old grizzly den."

Saunders nodded. "That's the straight."

"That was in the newspapers," Fargo interceded. "Let's ask Mr. Fargo here something that wasn't. F'rinstance, what did we drink when our canteens were empty?"

The Fargo on the ledge didn't miss a beat. "Why, the captain and me ate snow."

Saunders loosed a peal of derisive laughter. "In *July*?"

Grinning, the Mormon officer turned to Fargo. "Well, what did we drink?"

"We drank our own piss," Fargo replied bluntly. "We damn near puked it up. But somehow we held it down and were able to hang on another day."

"There you have it," Saunders announced. "No newspaper knew about that."

Fargo pointed at the criminal standing above them, whose face had turned to whey above the neat line of his beard. "I'd send a couple men topside, Captain. I wager you'll find two murdered men up in the Crow's Nest—Butch Landry and Orrin Trap. The third member of the gang was killed last night in the outlander camps—Harlan Perry. They hired this maggot to get even with me for landing them in prison. I expect you'll also find an actor's doodads up there: fake beards, wigs, and such truck."

"An actor's doodads?" the constable suddenly exclaimed.

"Great day in the morning! Men, I've got dodgers on this man. He's James Gramlich, alias Deets. Wanted in San Francisco for murdering an actress."

"Good work, Fargo," Deets said. "Drink *this* piss."

The Colt was only halfway out of the holster when Fargo's shooter, quicker than thought, leaped into his fist. He drilled Deets through the biceps; an eyeblink later Old Billy's bolos twirled rapidly through the air and wrapped the killer tight around the ankles. He was upended and went down hard on his ass. Several soldiers swarmed him.

"Nice shooting, Skye," Saunders congratulated him. "Thanks for not killing him."

"Kill him?" Fargo echoed, leathering his six-gun. "Captain, surely you jest? How could I kill a man that handsome?"

21

Twenty days after the events in Bingham Canyon, Skye Fargo and Old Billy Williams mapped the last line station for the Pony Express. The grueling Great Salt Desert and Sierra Madre Occidental lay behind them, and a pleasant ride through fertile fields and lush forest to the Pony Express office in Sacramento was crowned by drawing the balance of their pay.

"I s'pose you'll want me to buy your supper," Fargo remarked as the two men trotted their mounts down Union Street in downtown Sacramento.

"I was countin' on that," Old Billy admitted. "Hell, a steak is four bits in this Sodom. Six, happens you want trimmings."

Fargo shook his head in disbelief. "Christ, you piker, you just drew damn near four hundred dollars! Do you plan on burying it?"

"I do," Old Billy said from a deadpan face.

Fargo slanted a glance toward him. "That's straight goods?"

Old Billy nodded. "I bury any money I get. Got caches all over the West, from California to the Indian Territory."

"How the hell do you remember where they are?"

Billy tapped his temple with an index finger. "Mind maps. I'm damned if I'll mark them down on a real map. I can't write anyhow."

"But what the hell good are they? Money is like women—you get the most good out of them when you can touch them."

"This way, no matter where I go I always got money close to hand."

"But what good is it," Fargo pressed, "if you don't spend any of it?"

"Consarn it, Fargo, if I spend it I won't have it. Damn but you are thick in the head."

Fargo shook his head again and gave up. At the last trading post Old Billy had swapped an eagle-bone whistle for a plug of eating tobacco. Now he pulled it from his possibles bag and used his penknife to slice off a chaw. He parked it in his cheek and got it juicing good. Fargo knew what was coming and tried to suppress a grin.

"You say that oat-burner of yours is partic'lar about his ears?" Billy asked Fargo.

"He is that," Fargo replied, barely keeping a straight face.

"Good thing it's you in the saddle," Billy said, suddenly leaning sideways and loosing a brown streamer. The bulk of it splattered against the Ovaro's right ear.

The Ovaro gave a shrill whinny and went low, hunkering on his hocks. Old Billy roared with laughter, waiting to see the stallion chin the moon and toss Fargo ass over applecart.

Instead, the enraged horse snaked his powerful neck around and grabbed Old Billy's thick leather belt in his teeth. One whip of his head pulled the startled man from the saddle and tossed him fifteen feet to the left. Old Billy landed smack in a mud puddle. With an audible gulp he swallowed the tobacco in his mouth.

Fargo exploded with laughter and was forced to hold the saddle horn to keep from falling himself. Old Billy sat there sputtering, turning as purple as his birthmark.

"Fargo, you weasel-dick, chicken-plucking, sheep-humping dog from hell! That ain't no goddamn horse, it's a four-legged devil!"

"I tried to warn you," Fargo managed between fits of laughter. "My hand to God I did!"

Soon Billy, too, was suffering paroxysms of laughter. Passers-by stopped to stare at the two madmen. The laughter was infectious and before long everybody around them was laughing too. A sheriff's deputy hurried over to break it up but ended up laughing himself without even knowing why.

"Say," he called to the Trailsman, "ain't you Skye Fargo?"

"I am," the Trailsman replied, taking pleasure in saying it. "I really am."

LOOKING FORWARD!
The following is the opening section of the next novel in the exciting *Trailsman* series from Signet:

TRAILSMAN #362
RANGE WAR

The Guadalupes, New Mexico, 1859—
where lonely summits loom over a forbidding
land of the lawless.

Out of the dark mountains rose a howl that made the man by the campfire sit up and take notice. Loud and fierce, it was unlike any howl he'd ever heard. It echoed off the high peaks and was swept away by the wind into the black pitch of the night.

Broad of shoulder and narrow at the hips, Skye Fargo wore buckskins and a white hat turned brown with dust. A red bandanna, boots, and a well-used Colt at his hip completed his attire. He held his tin cup in both hands and glanced at his Ovaro. "What the hell was that?"

Fargo made his living as a scout, among other things. He'd wandered the West from Canada to Mexico and from the muddy Mississippi River to the broad Pacific Ocean. In his travels he'd heard hundreds of howling wolves and yipping coyotes and not a few wailing dogs, but he'd never, ever, heard anything like the cry that just startled him. More bray than howl, it was the most savage cry he'd ever heard.

Fargo settled back and sipped some coffee. Whatever it was, the thing was a ways off. He leaned back on his saddle.

"In a week we'll be in Dallas. Oats and a warm stall for you and a fine filly and whiskey for me."

The Ovaro had raised its head and pricked its ears at the howl. It looked at him and lowered its head to go back to dozing.

"Some company you are," Fargo said, and chuckled. He drained the tin cup and set it down.

By the stars it was pushing midnight. Fargo intended to get a good rest and be up at the crack of dawn. He was deep in the Guadalupe Mountains, high on a stark ridge that overlooked the Hermanos Valley. A ring of boulders hid his fire from unfriendly eyes.

This was Apache country, and outlaws were as thick as fleas on an old hound.

Fargo laced his fingers on his chest and closed his eyes. He was on the cusp of slumber when a second howl brought him to his feet with his hand on his Colt.

The howl was a lot closer.

The Ovaro raised its head again. It sniffed and stomped a hoof, a sure sign it had caught the animal's scent and didn't like the smell.

Fargo circled the fire to the stallion's side. He wasn't overly worried. Wolves rarely attacked people, and despite the strangeness of the howl, it had to be a wolf. He waited for a repeat of the cry, and when more than five minutes went by and the night stayed quiet, he shrugged and returned to his blankets and the saddle.

"I'm getting jumpy," he said to the Ovaro.

Pulling his hat brim low, Fargo made himself comfortable. He thought about the lady waiting for him in Dallas and the fine time they would have. She was an old acquaintance with a body as young and ripe as a fresh strawberry, and she loved to frolic under the sheets as much as he did. He couldn't wait.

Sleep claimed him. Fargo dreamed of Mattie and that body of hers. They were fit to bust a four-poster bed when another howl shattered the image. Instantly awake, he was out from under his blanket with the Colt in his hand before the howl died.

The short hairs at the nape of Fargo's neck pricked. The howl had been so close, he'd swear the thing was right on top of him.

The Ovaro was staring intently at a gap between two of the boulders.

Fargo sidled toward it. Warily, he peered out the opening, and broke out in gooseflesh.

A pair of eyes glared back at him. Huge eyes, like a wolf's, except that no wolf ever grew as large as the thing glaring at him. In the glow of the fire they blazed red like the eyes of a hell-spawned demon.

For all of ten seconds Fargo was riveted in disbelief. Then the red eyes blinked and the thing growled, and he shook himself and thumbed back the hammer. At the *click* the eyes vanished; they were there and they were gone, and he thought he heard the scrape of pads on rock.

Breathless, Fargo backed to the Ovaro. The thing might be after the stallion.

As the minutes crawled on claws of tension, and silence reigned, he told himself the thing must be gone.

Fargo reclaimed his seat. He added fuel to the fire and refilled his battered tin cup. He'd wait awhile before turning in.

From time to time Fargo had heard tales of wild animals bigger than most. Up in the geyser country there once roamed a grizzly the size of a log cabin, or so the old trappers who had been there liked to say. The Dakotas told a story about a white buffalo twice the size of any that ever breathed. Up Canada way, several tribes claimed that deep in the woods there lived hairy giants.

Fargo never gave much credence to any of the accounts. Tall tales were just that, whether related by white men or red men. He didn't believe in giants and goblins. But those eyes he saw didn't belong to any ordinary-sized critter.

Fargo shrugged and put them from his mind. The thing had gone. The Ovaro was safe, and he should get some sleep. He put down the cup and eased back on his saddle, but it was a long while before he succumbed. The slightest noise woke him with a start.

Then came a noise that wasn't so slight: a scream torn from a human throat.